See
Them
Die

"Who do you plan on shooting?"

"What?" asked Zip, the leader of the Latin Purples. "What did you say?"

"You handed an arsenal to those two kids. Who are you gonna shoot?" the sailor repeated.

"You got big eyes, Grandma," Zip said, and he struck the sailor full in the face with his closed fist as the rest of the gang moved up to join him. The sailor clutched for the countertop but his hand slid over the formica and he went over and back. He was struggling to get to his feet again when the first kick exploded against the side of his head. He brought up his hands instinctively, and the second kick caught him in the rib cage. Then the kicks started coming with methodical precision. A boot connected with his right eye and he felt shocking, stabbing pain and then the warmth of blood, and he thought I'm going to be kicked to death on the floor of this goddamn luncheonette, and then he heard a man shouting, "What are you doing? Bastards, what are you doing?" and above that, or beyond it, around it, circling it, filling the air, the high penetrating wail of a police siren. And then he heard no more . . .

Also by Ed McBain

Ghosts
Ten Plus One
He Who Hesitates

About the author

Ed McBain is one of the most illustrious names in
crime fiction and a holder of the Mystery Writers
of America's coveted Grand Master Award. He has
written more than eighty works of fiction, including
the heralded 87th Precinct series and the acclaimed
Matthew Hope series. His real name is Evan Hunter,
and he lives in Connecticut with his wife, Mary
Vann.

ED MCBAIN

See Them Die

A Novel of the 87th Precinct

CORONET BOOKS
Hodder and Stoughton

Copyright © 1960 by Ed McBain

The right of Ed McBain to be identified as the Author of
this work has been asserted by him in accordance with the
Copyright, Designs and Patents Act 1988.

First published in Great Britain in 1960 by Hamish Hamilton Ltd.
Published in Great Britain in 1994 by Hodder & Stoughton,
a division of Hodder Headline plc.

10 9 8 7 6 5 4 3 2

All rights reserved. No part of this publication may be
reproduced, stored in a retrieval system, or transmitted,
in any form or by any means without the prior written
permission of the publisher, nor be otherwise circulated
in any form of binding or cover other than that in which
it is published and without a similar condition being
imposed on the subsequent purchaser.

A CIP catalogue record for this title is available from
the British Library.

ISBN 0 340 59337 7

Typeset by Phoenix Typesetting, Ilkley, West Yorkshire.

Printed in Great Britain by
Cox & Wyman Ltd, Reading, Berkshire.

Hodder and Stoughton Ltd
A division of Hodder Headline PLC
338 Euston Road
London NW1 3BH

This is for Rita and Bud

The city in these pages is imaginary.
The people, the places, are all fictitious.
Only the police routine is based on established
investigatory technique.

1
—

July.

Heat.

In the city, they are synonymous, they are identical, they mean one and the same thing. In the 87th Precinct, they strut the streets with a vengeance, these twin bitches who wear their bleached blond hair and their bright-red lipstick slashes, who sway on glittering rhinestone slippers, who flaunt their saffron silk. Heat and July, they are identical twins who were born to make you suffer.

The air is tangible. You can reach out to touch it. It is sticky and clinging, you can wrap it around you like a viscous overcoat. The asphalt in the gutters has turned to gum, and your heels clutch at it when you try to navigate the streets. The pavements glow with a flat off-white brilliance, contrasting with the running black of the gutter, creating an alternating pattern of shade and light that is dizzying. The sun sits low on a still sky, a sky as pale as faded dungarees. There is only a hint of blue in this sky for it has been washed out by the intensity of the sun, and there is a shimmer over everything, the shimmer of heat ready to explode in rain.

The buildings bear the heat with the solemnity of Orthodox Jews in long, black frock coats. They have known this heat. Some of them have withstood it for close to a century, and so their suffering is a silent one; they face the heat with the intolerant blankness of stoics.

Scrawled onto the pavement in white chalk are the words: *JESÚS VIENE, PREPÁRENSE POR NUESTRA REDENCION!*

The buildings crowd the sidewalks and prepare neither for their redemption nor their perdition.

There is not much sky on this street.

There are places in the world where the sky is big, where it stretches from horizon to horizon like a gaudy blue tent, but such is not the case on this street. The sky here seems to have been wedged down over the uneven silhouette of the buildings, crammed into place because it would not fit properly, battered with a grimy fist until it tightly capped the street and contained the heat there.

The street is quiet.

It is only 8:40 in the morning, and it is Sunday.

There are unfluttering scraps of newspapers in the gutters; they share the gummy asphalt with empty tin cans and broken bottles and sticks ripped from orange crates. In the empty lot on one corner, there are the charred remains of bonfires, a torn and soiled crib mattress, the trailing white snakes of used condoms. The fire escapes are hung with the trivia of life: blankets, pillows, beer cases, potted plants, and here and there a guitar. A man sleeping on one of the fire escapes moves his arm, and it dangles down through the iron bars for a moment, swings idly, and then comes to a rest.

This is the only movement on the street.

The air is fetidly still. The heat is a self-contained, lifeless unit which does not stir and which discourages the motion of anything it embraces. It has baked itself into the brick fronts of the tenements, and the asphalt, and the pavements, and the sky. It has baked itself into these things and onto these things like orange enamel on copper.

Somewhere in the distance, the church bells toll, for this is Sunday morning, but even the bells ring out on the air with a harsh flatness, a metallic unevenness that must force its way through layers and layers of heat. Beneath that, like a rushing counterpoint, the elevated train roars past two blocks south, and then the train sound dies, and the bell sound dissipates in the sticky silence of the air, and the street is still once more.

Two people will die on this street today.

The boy's name was Zip.

He was seventeen years old and he erupted from the mouth of the tenement like a hand-grenade explosion. He came onto the stoop lightly, and then almost danced down the steps. He looked up at the waking man on the fire escape, waved nonchalantly, and then glanced up the street. He was tall and thin, good-looking in a craggy way, with a light complexion and black hair which he wore in a high crown off his forehead. He was wearing tight black slacks and high-topped combat boots and a bright silk purple jacket with his name embroidered in yellow on the left breast.

He looked at his watch.

It was 8:45, and he noted the time and then nodded, as if he had correctly estimated the exact duration of each of his movements up to this moment, as if he and the universe were meshing gears correctly. He looked up the street again. There was an air of restless urgency about him, the air a business magnate wears when he is expecting to close a deal for the purchase of a new company. The attitude was curious on a seventeen-year-old. And yet, he looked at his watch again, a person captured by the intricacies of time, the mind of a fifty-year-old banker seemingly ensnared in the body of an adolescent.

He lighted a cigarette, took several puffs on it, and then stamped it out under one booted foot. He looked at his watch again, stepped into the center of the street, and then started for the luncheonette on the corner. A huge sign traveled the corner of the building over the luncheonette like the marching electric letters of the Times Building in New York. These letters, however, were painted in red on a white field and they did not announce world-shattering events. They simply stated: LUIS LUNCHEONETTE. The luncheonette occupied a space in the corner of the building. When the doors were rolled back, the luncheonette became an extension of the sidewalk, open on both sides, the avenue and the street. The doors were closed now. The corrugated iron presented the impregnable look of a fortress. The boy went to the door on the street side, tried it, found it locked, and kicked it in anger.

"What are you doing there?" a voice said. "Get away from there!"

The man who came up the street had spoken with a slight Spanish accent, a gentle accent which seemed molded exactly to his appearance. He was a stoop-shouldered man wearing a small black mustache, a man who seemed older than his fifty-odd years, who moved with an economy that somehow seemed tortured.

"Don't tell me you're finally gonna open this dump!" Zip said.

Luís Amandez walked to the huge iron door and said, "What are you doing? Trying to break in here, hah? That what you were trying to do?"

He reached into his pocket for the key to the padlock, inserted it, took off the lock, and prepared to roll the door back into its overhead tracks.

"Don't flatter the dump," Zip said. "Come on, come on, get the lead out. Open the goddamn doors."

"This is my place, and I'll open them as slow or as fast as I want to. You snotnoses ..."

Zip grinned suddenly. "Come on, man," he said, and there was infectious warmth in his voice now. "You got to move! You want to get any place, you got to *move*."

Luís rolled back the first of the doors. "I wish *you* would move," he said. "To California."

"Dig the old bird," Zip said. "He's got humor." And he walked into the luncheonette and directly to the wall phone near the jukebox. Luís went around to the avenue side and took the padlock off the door there, rolling the door back, allowing the sunshine to rip through the corner stone like crossfire. Zip had taken the phone from its hook, reached into his pocket for a coin, and discovered that the smallest change he had was a quarter. He slammed the receiver onto the hook and went to meet Luís as he entered the shop.

"Listen, break a quarter for me," he said.

"What for?" Luís asked. "For the jukebox?"

"What's all the time 'What for?' Don't I buy enough in this crumby joint? I ask you for change, don't give me a Dragnet routine."

"It's too early to play the juke," Luís said calmly, going behind the counter and taking a white apron from a hook. "There are still people sleeping."

"In the first place, I don't care who's sleeping. It's time they were hustling. In the second place, I ain't gonna play the juke, I'm gonna make a phone call. And in the third and last place, you don't change this two bits for me, and one day you're liable to come in and find all your coffeepots busted."

"You threaten me?" Luís said. "I am a friend of the police. I tell them..."

"Come on, come on," Zip said, and again the warm grin flashed on his face. "You can sue me later. Right now, give me the change, huh? Come on."

Luís shook his head, picked up the quarter, and reached into his pocket. He made the change, and Zip picked it up and started for the telephone. He began dialing. Luís, since money matters had been brought to mind, walked to the cash register, reached into his pocket, and put in his day's starting money, laying the bills into the register drawer. He was about to break open a roll of dimes when Zip yelled, "Hey! Hey, Cooch! Over here!"

Luís turned. The second boy was also from the neighborhood, also wearing one of the purple silk jackets, but he was younger than Zip. Luís studied him from the distance of age, and wondered if he too had sported such a ridiculously thin and boyish-looking mustache when he was sixteen. He decided that he had not. The boy was short and squat, with thick powerful hands. His complexion was dark. He spotted Zip from the middle of the street and shouted, "Hey, Zipboy!" and then broke into a trot for the luncheonette. Luís sighed and cracked the roll of dimes on the edge of the cash drawer.

"What the hell kept you?" Zip asked. "I was just calling your house."

"Oh, man, don't ask," Cooch said. He spoke, as did Zip, without a trace of an accent. Both were total products of the city and the neighborhood, as far removed from Puerto Rico as was Mongolia. Studying them, Luís felt suddenly old, suddenly foreign. He shrugged, went to his stove, and began putting up his pots of coffee.

"My people are the eeriest, you know that, man?" Cooch said. He had large brown eyes, and he used his face expressively when he spoke, like a television comic going through a famous routine. "I think my old man must be on the Chamber of Commerce, I swear to God."

"What's your old man got to do with your being late? I said a quarter to nine, so here it is . . ."

"He gets a letter from Puerto Rico," Cooch went on blithely, "and right away he flips. 'Come stay with us,' he writes. 'Come live with us. Bring all your kids, and your grandma, and your police dog. We'll take care of you.'" Cooch slapped his forehead dramatically. "So all our goddamn barefoot cousins come flop with us. And every time another one shows up at the airport, my old man throws a party."

"Listen, what's this got to..."

"He threw a party last night. Out came the goddamn guitars. We had enough strings there to start a symphony. You shoulda seen my old man. He has a couple of drinks, right away his hands head for my old lady. Like homing pigeons. Two drinks, and his hands were on her ass."

"Look, Cooch, who cares *where* your old man's..."

"Judging from last night," Cooch said reflectively, "I should have another brother soon."

"All right, now how come you're late?"

"I been trying to tell you. The jump didn't break up until four A.M. I could hardly crawl outa bed this morning. I still can't see too straight." He paused. "Where's Papá? Ain' he here yet?"

"That's what I'm wondering. You all think we're playing games here."

"Who, me?" Cooch said, offended. "Me? *I* think that?"

"Okay, maybe not you," Zip said, relenting. "The other guys."

"Me?" Cooch persisted, astonished and hurt. "Me? Who was it first showed you around the scene when you moved up here?"

"Okay, I said not you, didn't I?"

"Where'd you come from? Some crumby slum near the Calm's Point Bridge? What the hell did you know about this neighborhood? Who showed you around, huh?"

"You did, you did," Zip said patiently.

"Yeah. So right away you hop on me. A few minutes late, and you..."

"*Ten* minutes late," Zip corrected.

"All right, ten minutes, I didn't know you had a stop watch. Man, I don't understand you sometimes, Zip. Saying I think we're playing games here. Man, if ever a guy..."

"I said not you! For Pete's sake, I said *not you!* I'm talking about the other studs." He paused. "Did you stop by for Sixto?"

"Yeah. That's another reason I'm late. You give me all these stops to..."

"So where is he?"

"He had to help his old lady."

"Doing what?"

"With the baby. Listen, you think it's kicks having a baby in the house? I never seen a kid could wet her pants like Sixto's sister. Every time you turn around, that kid is pissing."

"He was changing her pants?" Zip asked, astonished.

"He was powdering her behind the last time I seen him."

"I'm gonna powder *his* behind when he gets here!" Zip said angrily. "See, that's just what I mean. He thinks we're fooling around here. Then you wonder why we ain't making a name for ourselves. It's because nobody on this club's for real, that's why. Everybody expects me to do everything."

"We got a name, Zip," Cooch said gently.

"We got balls! You guys still think this is a goddamn basket ball team at the Boys' Club. When you gonna grow up? You want to walk the streets in this neighborhood, or you want to hide every time there's a backfire?"

"I don't hide from nothing!"

"You think anybody on the Royal Guardians is scared of anything?" Zip asked.

"No, but the Royal Guardians got two hundred and fifty members."

"So how do you think they got them members? By being late when there's a wash job scheduled?"

"Hey!" Cooch said suddenly.

"What's the matter?"

"Shhhh."

A woman was coming up the street, her ample breasts bobbing with the haste of her steps. Her black hair was pulled into a bun at the back of her neck. She looked neither to the right nor to the left. She walked with a purposefulness, almost a blindness, passing the boys who stood in the open street side of the luncheonette, turning the corner, and moving out of sight.

"You see who that was?" Cooch whispered.

"That lady?"

"Yeah." Cooch nodded. "Alfie's mother."

"What?" He walked to the corner and stared up the avenue. But the woman was already gone.

"Alfredo Gomez's mother," Cooch said. "Man, was she in a hurry! Zip, you think he told her?"

"What do I care, he told her or not?"

"What I mean ... like this is his old lady ... like if he told her ..."

"So he told her. How's that gonna help him?"

"You know how dames are. She might've got excited. She might've ..."

"Stop crapping your pants, will you? You got nothing but small-time guts, you know that? You're just like my old man. He talks like a senator. A real wheel. Always telling me about Puerto Rico. Who cares about that damn island? I was born here, right in this city. I'm a *real* American. But he's always telling me what a big shot he was in San Juan. You know what it turns out he done there? I found out from one of my uncles. You know what he done?"

"What?"

"He fixed bicycles for a living. So that's the big wheel. Big *talk* that's all. But small-time guts."

"I got as much guts ..."

"Sure, so you see Alfie's mother out for a stroll, and you start shaking. You know what you're gonna be when you grow up?"

"No. What?"

"A guy who fixes bicycles."

"Aw, come on. I..."

"Or a guy who shines shoes."

"I never shined a pair of shoes in my life!" Cooch said proudly. "I don't even shine my *own* shoes!"

"That's why you look like a slob," Zip said, and then abruptly turned his head. Someone was approaching.

2

The sailor had rounded the corner as Cooch spoke. He was a tall, blond man – well, not exactly a man, and yet not a boy. He was perhaps twenty-two years old, and he had reached that mysterious boundary line which divided a man from a boy, but he was still straddling the line so that it was impossible to think of him as a boy, and yet stretching a point to consider him a man. Man or boy, he was quite drunk at the moment. He walked with the sailor's habitual roll, but the roll was somewhat frustrated by his erratic drunken weaving. His white hat was perched precariously on the back of his head, and his white uniform was spotlessly clean, reflecting the early-morning sunshine with a dazzling brilliance. He stopped on the corner, looked up at the sign over the luncheonette, mumbled something to himself, shook his head violently, and then continued up the street.

Zip stifled a laugh and nudged Cooch in the ribs.

"Ten bucks says I know what he's looking for," Cooch said, grinning.

"Never mind what he's looking for. Go get Sixto and Papá.

Tell them I'm waiting, and tell them I'm getting slightly p.o.'d. Now move."

"Don't get excited," Cooch said, but he moved up the street quickly, passing the drunken sailor who had headed back towards the luncheonette. The sailor was in that sort of haze where everything seems to involve a decision meriting vast concentration and deliberation. He stopped at each building, studied the numerals, shook his head solemnly, and finally wound up in front of the luncheonette again, still shaking his head. He studied the sign, considered the vast symbolism in the words LUIS LUNCHEONETTE, pondered this symbolism for a while, shook his head again, and was beginning to retrace his steps down the street when Zip said, "Help you, sailor?"

"Huh?" the sailor asked.

"You look lost," Zip said. His manner was quite pleasant. He grinned warmly and the sailor responded to the grin immediately, the lost wanderer accepting the first friendly hand.

"Listen," he said drunkenly, "where's La ... La Galli ... La ... Listen, I was talking to a guy inna bar downtown, you know? An' we began discussin' ..." He stopped and studied Zip with drunkenly profound narrowness. "Listen, how old are you?"

"Seventeen," Zip said.

"Oh."

The sailor tabulated this silently, his mind whirring. He nodded. "Okay, then. I didn't wanna impair the morals of a ... so this guy an' me, we were discussin' ... well, I was sorta expressin' my desire for sorta climbin' into bed with a female, you know? A girl. You know?"

"So he sent you up here?"

"Yeah. No. Yeah, yeah, he did. He said there was a place up here called ... ah ... La Gallina." He pronounced the word with a Western twang that brought a new smile to Zip's mouth.

"*La Gallina*, yes," Zip said, giving it the proper Spanish pronunciation.

"Yeah," the sailor said, nodding, "where he said I could get anything I want. Now how about that?"

"He was right," Zip answered.

"So here I am," the sailor said. He paused. "Where is it?"

"Right down the street there."

"Thank you," the sailor said, nodding. "Thank you ver' much." He started off down the street again.

"Don't mention it," Zip said, smiling. He stared after the sailor for a few moments, and then went into the luncheonette. "Give me a cup of coffee, Luís," he said.

The sailor went down the street, studying each doorway as he had before. He stopped suddenly, looked at the lettering on the plate-glass window of a bar, and muttered, "La Gallina, I'll be damned. Feller was right." He walked directly to the front door, not expecting it to be locked, trying to open it, and then discovering that it was locked, immensely annoyed that the knob had resisted his hand. He backed away from the door and yelled, "Hey! Hey, wake up! Wake up, goddamnit! I'm here!"

"What the hell is that?" Luís said.

"Sailor out there," Zip said, grinning.

Luís came from behind the counter. Up the street, the sailor was still shouting at the top of his lungs.

"You!" Luís said. "Quiet, quiet."

The sailor turned. "You talking to me, mate?"

"*Sí*, I'm talking to you, mate. Stop the racket. This is Sunday morning. People like to sleep, you know? You wake them up."

"Well, hell, thass what I'm *trying* to do, you know."

"Why you trying to wake them up for?"

"'Cause I wanna go to bed."

"That makes sense, all right," Luís said, nodding patiently. "Are you drunk?"

"Me?" the sailor said. "Me?"

"Yes."

"Hell, no."

"You look perhaps a little drunk."

The sailor walked to where Luís was standing, put his hands on his hips and said, "Well, maybe I am perhaps a li'l drunk. So ain't you never been perhaps a li'l drunk?"

"I have been a little drunk," Luís said, "and I have been a lot drunk. Come. I'll make you a cup of coffee."

"Whuffor?"

"What for?" Luís shrugged and walked into the luncheonette. The sailor followed him. "Because I like sailors," Luís said. "I used to be a sailor myself once."

"Did you find it, pal?" Zip interrupted.

"Yeah. It's closed."

"I coulda told you that."

"So why dinn you?"

"You didn't ask."

"Oh, you're one of *those* guys," the sailor said.

"Which guys?" Zip asked, and he stiffened suddenly on the counter stool, as if expecting an attack.

"The guys you got to ask."

"Yeah," Zip answered. "I'm one of *those* guys. So what?"

Rapidly, perhaps because he sensed Zip's sudden belligerence, perhaps because he simply wanted to switch the conversation back to himself, Luís said, "Yes, I was in the Navy from 1923 to 1927. Yes, sir."

"Was you on a ship?" the sailor asked. If he had detected any challenge in Zip's voice, he was studiously ignoring it. Either that, or he was too drunk to have noticed.

"A man who has not been on a ship is not a sailor." He looked over at the bubbling Silexes. "The coffee is almost ready."

"What kind of a ship?"

"A garbage scow," Zip said quickly, and he grinned.

"Never mind this smart one. I was on a mine sweep."

"What was your rate?" the sailor asked suspiciously.

"You never heard of Rear Admiral Luís Amandez?" Zip

asked, mock surprise spreading over his uneven features.

"I was a steward's mate," Luís answered with dignity. "And you shut up, you little snotnose."

"Wha'd he say your name was? Louise?"

"Yeah, that's right," Zip answered, chuckling. "This here is Aunt Louise."

"Louise? Yeah?"

"No, Luís. Luís."

"No, Louise," Zip insisted.

"Are you a Mexican, Louise?" the sailor asked.

"No." Luís shook his head. "Puerto Rican."

"Well, that's the same thing, ain't it?"

"Well—" Luís thought for a moment, and then shrugged resignedly. "*Sí*, the same thing."

"What part of Mehico you from?" the sailor asked obliviously.

"The part down in the Caribbean," Luís said dryly.

"The annex," Zip put in. "South. You know?"

"And whereabouts in Puerto Rico?"

"A town called Cabo Rojo, do you know it?"

"I only know Tia Juana," the sailor said, "and I ain't even been *there*. Closest I ever got was San Diego."

"Here," Luís said, pouring a cup of coffee. "Drink this."

"Where's mine?" Zip asked.

"I have only two hands." He finished pouring the sailor's coffee, and then poured a cup for Zip.

"What brung you all the way here from Puerto Rico?" the sailor asked.

"Work," Luís said. "A man has to work, you know."

"Where *you* from, sailor?" Zip asked.

"Fletcher," the sailor said. "That's in Colorado."

"I never heard of it."

"It's there, all right."

The three fell silent.

Zip and the sailor sipped at their coffee. Luís got to work behind the counter. There seemed to be nothing more

to say to each other. The three, after all, had very little
in common. One had inquired about the whereabouts of
a bar-quasi-whorehouse. The other had told him where it
was. The third had served them both coffee. One was in
his early fifties, the other was perhaps twenty-two, and
the third was seventeen. One was born in Puerto Rico, the
other in Fletcher, Colorado, and the third was a native
of the city. Thus divided by time and space and natural
inclination, there was nothing each could say to the other
at the moment, and so they fell silent.

And yet, within the silence, their thoughts ran in strangely
similar patterns so that, if the thoughts had been voiced,
each would have instantly understood – or thought he'd
understood – the other.

Luís had begun thinking about why he'd come to the
mainland, about why he'd left the place of his birth. He
had told the sailor he had come here to work, and yet
he knew it was something more than that. It was not to
work, it was to *begin*. He had lived on the island with a
wife and three children, and the island – despite his love
for it – had meant primarily one thing, and that thing was
hunger. Constant hunger. Hunger that lingered through the
cane-cutting season because you could not spend all of your
earnings while the season was in swing; you had to save
some for the empty days ahead. There was not much to
hold and not much to save. You fished in the off season, and
sometimes your haul was good – but most of the time you
were hungry. And being hungry, even knowing that everyone
else around you was hungry, being hungry somehow reduced
you to being nothing. There were things he would always love
about the island, the innate pride and decency and hospitality
of the people, the respect humans automatically showed to
other humans, a respect bred of sunshine and lush tropical
foliage where cruelty seemed blatantly out of place. The island
seemed to draw people closer together, strengthening their

bonds as humans. And yet, contradicting this was the dire economic need, so that on the one hand Luís had felt like a very important person with many friends and much love, and on the other he had felt like a hungry animal.

And so he'd left the island. He'd left the island in search of a beginning. He had worked hard for the luncheonette. It was still owned mostly by the bank, but he knew now that he would never go hungry again. And if he had lost something else, something quite dear to him, he had another sort of satisfaction, and this satisfaction was in his stomach and his bowels where perhaps a man feels it most.

The sailor sipped at his coffee and thought of Fletcher, Colorado.

He did not often think of Fletcher because he found he got sad whenever he did. He had been born in Fletcher, and he learned early the meaning of the words "small town". When a place is called a small town, it has nothing whatever to do with the size of the town. A giant metropolis can be a small town, and some very large cities *are* small towns in every sense of the word. Fletcher, Colorado, was just like every other small town in the United States of America. There was a schoolhouse, and a church, and a row of stores. There were DRIVE – CHILDREN – SLOW signs, and SPEED LIMIT STRICTLY ENFORCED signs, and there were the teenage kids hanging out in the corner drugstore, and the Boy Scout cookouts, and the Little League, and the choir practice, and the *Saturday Evening Post* route, and in the spring the forsythias lined the highway with bright yellow and there was the bursting pink of cherry blossoms, and in the fall he would go hunting for deer with his father and his older brother, and the woods would shriek with color. In the winter, there was deep snow and skiing. The mountains surrounded the town. You could always see the mountains. Everybody in town knew everybody else in town.

He met Corrine at a church picnic when he was six years old. By the time they were eleven, everybody in town had decided that one day they would get married. When he got a swimming medal in his freshman year at high school, he gave it to Corrine. He went everywhere with Corrine and did everything with Corrine, and it became plain to him after a while that Corrine was perfectly happy to have been born and raised in a town like Fletcher, and that she would be happy to get married there, and breed kids there, and eventually to die there. And suddenly, he wondered if this was what he himself wanted.

Oh, he loved Corrine, it wasn't that. He supposed he loved her. She had very straight red hair that she wore loose around her shoulders, and she had very bright blue eyes and a nose that tilted slightly at the tip, she looked exactly like those pictures of small-town American girls he had seen on the covers of the *Saturday Evening Post* when he used to deliver the magazine. And he liked to neck with her. He liked to touch her, too, whenever she let him, which wasn't often, and he never could figure out when she wanted him to and when she didn't want him to; he supposed he loved her because he respected her wishes in the matter.

And then, one day, all of a sudden, he decided he was going to join the Navy. When his parents asked him why, when Corrine asked him why, when his friends asked him why, he told them he would be drafted soon anyway, and he might just as well go into the Navy where a fellow didn't have to go on hikes or sleep in the mud. That was what he told all these people. But he knew why he was really joining the Navy. He was joining the Navy to get out of Fletcher. He was joining the Navy because Fletcher was slowly and surely suffocating him, and he could feel those mountains moving in closer and closer every day, and he knew that one day he would no longer be able to breathe, that one day he would be crushed by everything in this small town. When he left, he told himself he would never return. And so it made him sad to think about Fletcher.

Zip, drinking his coffee, studying his reflection in the mirror behind the counter, did not feel sad at all. Zip felt pretty damn good. Zip felt, at last, that things were beginning to click. They had never clicked for him in that ratty neighborhood downtown. There'd been nothing there for him but getting kicked by the older kids. Fat Ass Charlie, they used to call him. Fat Ass Charlie, and *bam!* a well-placed kick right in the middle of that fat ass. The nickname had persisted even when he began thinning into adolescence. And then they'd moved.

And suddenly, he wasn't fat-assed any more, and he wasn't even Charlie any more. He began calling himself Zip, and he began feeling that there was opportunity in this new neighborhood, the opportunity to be the person he wanted to be, and not the person everybody else thought he should be. He'd met Cooch, and Cooch had shown him the ropes and suggested that they join the biggest club in the neighborhood, the Royal Guardians.

But Zip had ideas of his own. Why become a schnook running around the fringes of the higher-ups when you could have a club of your own? And so he suggested the Latin Purples, and he planned to start it small, six, seven guys to begin with – so far there were only four. And Cooch's sister-in-law had sewn the purple jackets for them, and he wore his jacket with a great deal of pride now because the jacket meant something to him, the jacket meant that he was on his way.

If you'd asked him where he was going, he couldn't have told you.

But he knew he was on his way, and he knew that today would be the clincher, today would be the day he realized himself fully as a person.

And so the three of them sat with their separate thoughts, thoughts which were strangely similar, and when the sailor finally spoke, both Luís and Zip knew instantly what he meant.

The sailor said, "You can lose yourself in Fletcher. You

can get just plumb lost." He shook his head. "That's why I left. I wanted to know who I was."

"And have you found out?" Luís asked.

"Give him time," Zip said. "You think a guy can make a rep in one day?"

"I'll find out, Louise," the sailor said.

"How? With the girls from La Gallina?"

"Huh?"

"Sailor, take my advice," Luís said. "Go back to your ship. This neighborhood is not always a nice place."

"Leave him alone," Zip said. "He wants a girl, I'll help him find one." He winked at the sailor, and then he grinned broadly.

"Don't let Sunday morning fool you," Luís said. "Last night, there was drinking and guitars. And this morning, everyone sleeps. But sometimes ... sailor, take my advice. Go back to your ship ..."

"I think I'll hang around for a while."

"Then be careful, eh? You are a stranger here. Choose your company." He looked at Zip meaningfully. "There are good and bad, *entiende?* You understand? Take care."

The sailor swung around on his stool. He leaned his elbows on the counter top and drunkenly looked out over the sun-washed street.

"It looks nice and peaceful to me," he murmured.

"Can you see through the walls, sailor?" Luís asked. "Do you know what goes on under the skin of the buildings?"

3

The skin of the building which housed the uniformed cops and detectives of the 87th Precinct was not lovely, nor engaged, nor had it been washed in more than half a century. It presented a characterless gray to the park across the street, a gray which seemed contradictory to the bright sunshine that filled the air. The gray stones were rough and uneven, covered with the soot and grime of the city, relieved only by the hanging green globes which announced in white numerals to the world at large that this was Precinct 87.

The low, flat steps of the front stoop led to a pair of glass-fronted doors which were open now to permit the entrance of whatever scant breeze rustled across Grover Park. The breeze, unfortunately, did not get very much further than the entrance doors. It certainly did not pass into the muster room where Sergeant Dave Murchison sat behind his high desk pulling at his undershorts and cursing the heat. A rotating electric fan sat on top of the switchboard to the left of the desk. The switchboard, at the moment, wasn't blinking with calls from the violated citizenry, thank God. Murchison wiped sweat from his brow, tugged at his undershorts, and wondered if it was any cooler upstairs.

A long wooden plaque, painted white and then overlaid with the black letters DETECTIVE DIVISION, pointed to a flight of narrow iron-runged steps which led upstairs to the bull pen. The flight of steps, gathering heat only from a small window where the steps turned back upon themselves before continuing to the second floor, was perhaps the coolest spot in the station house. Beyond the steps, a long corridor led to the detective squadroom where a battery of electric fans fought valiantly to produce some semblance of a breeze. The grilled windows at the far end of the squadroom admitted bright, golden sunlight which spread across the wooden floor like licking flames. The men in the squadroom sat in shirt sleeves at sun-drenched desks.

If there was one nice thing about being a detective, it was the fact that a gray flannel suit, a button-down shirt, and a neat black tie were not requisites of the job. Detective Steve Carella was perhaps the only detective in the squadroom on that Sunday morning in July who looked as if he might be an advertising executive. But then, Carella always looked as if he were dressed for the pages of *Esquire*. Even wearing a leather jacket and dungarees, he managed to exude the scent of careful grooming. He was a tall man whose sinewy body gave only the slightest hint of the power he possessed. Unpadded, slender with a rawboned simplicity, he seemed built to flatter whatever clothes were heaped onto his frame. This morning he was wearing a blue seersucker suit, the jacket of which was draped over the back of his chair. He had worn a bow tie to work, but had untied it the moment he entered the squadroom so that it hung loosely about his neck now, his shirt unbuttoned, his head bent over the report he was studying.

The other cops presented a slightly less sartorial appearance. Andy Parker, a cop who would have looked like a bum even when dressed for his own funeral, was wearing a pair of tan nylon slacks and a sports shirt which had surely been designed in honor of Hawaii's having achieved statehood. Hula girls swayed their hips all over Parker's shirt. Surfboarders flitted over his huge barrel chest. The colors on the shirt exploded like Roman candles. Parker, who looked unshaven even though he had shaved closely before reporting to the squadroom, pounded at a typewriter with both huge hands, using his fingers like fists. The typewriter seemed to resist each successive assault wave, a machine refusing to succumb to brute force. Parker continued to smash into it as if he were engaged in mortal combat, cursing each time the keys locked, slamming the carriage over whenever he reached the end of a line of the D.D. report, the bell clanging savagely in protest.

"No arrest," he muttered savagely, "but I got to type up a damn report, anyway."

"Be glad you're alive," Carella said, not looking up from the sheet in his hands.

"It'll take more than a punk like Pepe Miranda to put the blocks to me, pal," Parker said. He continued smashing at the typewriter.

"You're lucky," Carella said. "He was feeling charitable. He had your gun, and he had everybody else's gun, and you're just damn lucky he didn't decide to kill you all."

"He was chicken," Parker said, looking up. "If that was me in his place, I'd have blasted every cop in sight, and then shot a few passers-by just for the hell of it. But Miranda was chicken. He knows the jig's up, so he figured he wouldn't add anything else to what we already got on him."

"Maybe he liked your face," Carella said. "Maybe he figured you were too sweet to shoot."

"Yeah," Parker said, and he ripped the D.D. report from the machine. He did not like Carella. He could still remember the time in March when he and Carella had mixed it up a little in the squadroom. The fight had ended abruptly because Frankie Hernandez had reminded them both that the lieutenant was in the building. But Parker didn't like unfinished business. And maybe Carella had forgotten all about the incident – though he doubted it – but Parker had not, and would not until the thing was resolved finally, one way or another. Thinking back to that March day, he thought it odd that the same men had been present in the squadroom, the three of them, and that Carella had taken offense at a chance remark made to Hernandez. Why the hell were people always so touchy? He dropped the report on his desk and walked to the water cooler.

Frankie Hernandez, the third man who'd been there on that March day, the third man in the squadroom on this day in July, was standing at one of the filing cabinets, the drawer open. He wore a short-sleeved white shirt and dark-blue trousers. A .38 police special protruded from the holster strapped to his chest. He was a wide-shouldered man with a tan complexion and straight, black hair. His eyes were brown, the eyes of man who expected to be offended and who, as a result, was constantly prepared for the eventuality. It was not easy to be a Puerto Rican cop in a neighborhood with such a large Puerto Rican population – especially if you happened to have been born and raised in the streets of the precinct. Whatever battles Hernandez fought with his neighbors, the police, and himself were reflected in his eyes. He was not a happy man. No man dedicated to a single cause ever is.

"What do you think of your pal there?" Parker asked from the cooler.

"What pal?" Hernandez asked

"Miranda."

"He's no pal of mine," Hernandez answered.

"I thought we had him cold yesterday," Parker said, filling a paper cup and drinking from it. He wiped his lips with the back of his hand. "Five of us walked into that apartment, and the son of a bitch pulls a gun from someplace up his sleeve and cold-cocks us. The rotten punk. He made us look like amateurs. You see the paper today? 'Miranda Foils Cops.' A punk getting headlines."

"He's still no pal of mine," Hernandez said.

"Yeah," Parker answered. He seemed ready to say more, but he let the matter drop. "Who was that woman up here?" he asked.

"Her name's Gomez," Hernandez answered.

"What'd she want?"

"Her son's in some kind of trouble. She wants me to talk to him."

"What the hell does she think you are? A priest?"

Hernandez shrugged.

"You gonna go?" Parker asked.

"As soon as I finish what I'm working on."

"Maybe you are a priest."

"Maybe," Hernandez replied.

Parker walked to the coat rack in one corner of the room and took a dark-blue Panama from one of the pegs. "I'm going outside," he said, "see if I can't hear something."

"About what?" Carella asked.

"About that punk Miranda. He didn't vanish into thin air, that's for sure. So where would you go if you was him?"

"To Russia," Carella replied.

"Yeah. Well, I think he came back here. Right here someplace. He sure as hell wouldn't try to find another pad in Riverhead, not after we almost collared him there. So where? Home. Home to the 87th. And if he's somewhere around here, you can bet your ass everybody in the streets knows just where. So Andy Parker goes on the earie." He stopped at his desk, opened the top drawer, took out his service revolver and holster, and clipped the holster into his right hip pocket. "Don't work too hard," he said, as he went through the gate in the railing. "Not that I think you need the advice."

His footsteps echoed down the long corridor. Hernandez watched him as he turned to go down the flight of iron-runged steps. When he looked back into the squadroom, he saw that Carella had been watching the other man, too.

A glance passed between them. Neither said a word. Silently, they got back to work.

Azucena Gomez had been one of those fortunate people who are born beautiful and who remain beautiful no matter what tricks life decides to play on them. Her name, translated from the Spanish, meant White Lily, and she seemed to have been appropriately named because her skin was white and smooth, and her face, her body, seemed to combine all the delicate beauty and regality of that flower. The oval of her face was dominated by brown eyes which slanted to lend an exotic flair to otherwise serene features. Her nose was straight and slender, her mouth was a mouth which looked as if it could cry. She had managed, without the benefit of dieting, to maintain a body which had evoked many a street-corner whistle in her native Puerto Rico. She was forty-two years old, and she had known what it was to be a woman, still knew, and she knew the happiness and sorrow of motherhood. She was not a tall woman, perhaps the one flaw which robbed her of true beauty, but she seemed exceptionally tall as she stood by the bed and looked down at her son.

"Alfredo?" she said.

He did not answer her. He lay on the bed full length, his face buried in the pillow.

"Alfredo?"

He did not look up. He did not turn his head from the pillow. "Mama, lee me alone," he mumbled. "Please."

"You have to listen to me," she said. "It is important that you listen to me."

"It don' make no difference wha' you say, Mama. I already know what I got to do."

"You must go to the church, is that what you must do?"

"*Sí.*"

"And they will harm you."

He sat up suddenly. He was a sixteen-year-old boy with his mother's fair complexion and wide, brown eyes. The slight fuzz of adolescence clung to his cheeks. His mouth, like his mother's seemed ready to twist into sorrow.

"I go to church every Sunday," he said simply. "I go today too. They cannot stop me."

"They cannot stop you, but they will harm you. Is this what they said?"

"*Sí.*"

"Who told you this?"

"The boys."

"Which boys?"

"Mama, this is not for you," Alfredo said plaintively. "This is somethin'..."

"Why? Why will they hurt you?"

Alfredo would not answer. He stared at his mother, but he remained silent.

"Why, Alfredo?"

The tears came suddenly. He felt them welling into his eyes, and he turned from her quickly so that she would not see him crying. He threw himself onto the bed again, his face buried in the pillow, his shoulders heaving as he sobbed. His mother touched his shoulder.

"Cry," she said.

"Mama, I am asha—"

"It is good to cry. Your father used to cry sometimes. It is not a sin for a man to cry."

"Mama, Mama, please, you don't understan'..."

"I understand that you are my son," Mrs. Gomez said with simple logic. "I understand that you are good, and that those who wish to harm you are bad. It is not for the bad ones to rule the streets, Alfredo. You say you must go to eleven o'clock mass, the way you always do. You say you must go, even though they will hurt you. *This* I do *not* understand."

He sat up again, and the words sprang from his lips like a scream.

"*I cann turkey out!*"

"You can't ... turkey out?" she asked, puzzled.

"I cann be afray, Mama. I cann be turkey. You don' understan'. This is not somethin' you understan'. Please. Let me do what I got to do."

His mother stood by the bed, staring at him, staring at her son as if somehow she did not know him any longer, as if somehow the infant she had held to her breast, the infant who had sucked of her milk was no longer someone she knew. His face, his language, even his eyes seemed distant and strange. She studied him as if trying to force the reconstruction of an earlier bond through the power of her eyes alone.

At last she said, "I have gone to the police."

"What!" he shouted.

"*Sí.*"

"Why did you do that? You think the police will care abou' me? About Alfredo Gomez? The police are no good. Don' you know the police here in this neighborhood?"

"There are good police and bad police. I have gone to Frankie Hernandez."

"He iss the same as dee ress. Mama, why did you do this? Why cann you stay out of this?"

"Frankie will help you. He is from the *barrio.*"

"But he's a cop now, a detective. He ..."

"He grew up here in these streets. He is Spanish, and he helps his people. He will help you."

"You shoul' not have gone," Alfredo said, shaking his head.

"I have never been inside a police station in my life," Mrs. Gomez said. "Today is the first time. My son is in danger, and I went for help." She paused. "He said he would come.

I gave him the address. He said he would come to talk to you."

"I will tell him nothing," Alfredo said softly.

"You will tell him all that is necessary to tell him."

"Wha' time is it?" he asked suddenly.

"You have time yet."

"I got to dress for church."

"Not until you talk to Frankie Hernandez. He will know what to do."

"He will know what to do," Alfredo said. "Sure, he will know what to do," and the mockery in his voice was tinged with bitterness and inescapable sorrow.

"He will know what to do," Mrs. Gomez said confidently.

4

The sailor's name was Jeff Talbot, and the rosy glow of the alcohol was beginning to wear off, and as he surveyed the street outside the luncheonette, he wondered how he could ever have said it looked like a nice neighborhood. Somehow, even the sunlight did not help the look of the street outside. It helped only in the way a powerful spotlight helps to illuminate a garbage dump. He blinked at the sunshine, and he blinked at the street outside, and he suddenly said, "I'm sober," and just as suddenly realized that he was.

"Good," Luís said. "How does the world look?"

"Miserable." He swung his stool back toward the counter. "I'm getting a headache. This is a pretty rotten neighborhood, ain't it?"

"It depends how you look at it," Zip said. "I happen to like it."

"You do?"

"It's where I live. When I'm here, that sidewalk sings."

"What does it sing?" Jeff asked. His head was beginning to pound. He wondered why he was talking with a stranger, wondered why he'd drunk so much the night before.

"With him," Luís said, "it sings Rock and Roll."

"The old man is very hip, sailor. He knows all the proper ..."

Zip stopped talking. He tensed suddenly on the stool, his eyes fastened to the street outside.

"What's the matter?" Jeff asked.

"The Law," Zip said quietly.

The Law to which he had referred was the law as personified by Detective Andy Parker who walked up the street with a sort of slumped, indifferent swagger, a cigarette dangling from the corner of his mouth, looking for all the world like a penniless bum who had just come from sleeping one off in a doorway. His bright Hawaiian shirt was rumpled and soiled with coffee stains. He scratched his chest indolently, his eyes flicking the street as he walked.

"The only law I got to worry about is the Shore Patrol," Jeff said, dismissing him. He shoved his empty cup across the counter. "Can I get another cup of joe?" He grinned and then winced in pain. "Oh, man, but that head hurts when I smile."

Outside the luncheonette, Andy Parker waved at Luís and said, "*Qué pasa, maricón?*"

"Hello, Andy," Luís said, smiling. "Some coffee?"

"I can use a cup," Parker answered. "Hot." He walked into the luncheonette and took the stool next to Jeff's. He studied Zip for a moment and then asked, "When did you start catering to the punk trade, Luís?"

"I'm having a cup of coffee," Zip answered. "Anything wrong with that, Lieutenant?"

"I ain't a lieutenant, and don't get smart."

"I thought you'd at least be a captain by now. After all the drunks you pulled in from Grover Park."

"Look, kid ..."

"This is Detective Andy Parker, sailor," Zip said. "He's what is known as a tough cop. Fearless. For two cents, he'd arrest his own grandmother." He grinned almost immediately, and Jeff recognized the pattern suddenly. It was as if someone had advised the boy that a grin would take him a long way, especially a grin composed of such sparkling white teeth, a grin that never failed to generate a warm response in its recipient. Even Parker, faced with the sudden dazzling brilliance of the grin, smiled.

"For two cents," he answered, "I'd kick your ass all over the sidewalk." But there was no menace in his words. The threat, disarmed by the grin, was a hollow one.

"See?" Zip said, still grinning. "I'll bet he can lick any sixteen-year-old kid on the block."

"Go ahead," Parker said, "push me another inch, kid." But again the threat was not real, the smile had stolen all its power. He turned his attention to the sailor, studied him for a moment and then said, "What are you doing around here, sailor?"

"Same thing as the kid here," Jeff answered. "Having a cup of coffee."

"Let's try it again," Parker said tiredly. "What are you doing around here?"

"I heard you the first time," Jeff said.

"Then give me a straight answer."

"Is this neighborhood off limits?"

"No, it ain't off limits, but it sure as hell..."

"Then leave me alone."

Parker studied him silently for a moment. Then he said, "Pretty salty, huh?"

"Yeah, pretty salty," Jeff said.

"Andy, he's a little drunk," Luís put in, spreading his hands. "You know, go easy on..."

"Keep out of this, Luís," Parker snapped.

"I'm sober now, Louise. Thanks."

"I asked a question."

"Oh, for God's sake," Jeff said, "I came to sit up with a sick grandmother."

Zip burst out laughing and then immediately squelched the laughter when Parker turned a frigid glare on him. Zip shrugged. Parker turned back to the sailor.

"What's your grandmother's name?" he asked icily.

"Now you got me, officer. I always just called her plain Grandma."

"What ship you off?"

"Why?"

"I'm asking!"

"How do I know you ain't a Russian spy?"

"You guys think you're pretty wise, don't you? Coming up here and fouling up my precinct?"

"Who's fouling up your lousy precinct? I'm drinking a cup of coffee, that's all."

"Here, Andy, here," Luís said, anxious to make peace. "Here's *your* coffee. Drink it while it's still hot."

Parker took the cup. "You know how many sailors get rolled up here?" he persisted.

"How many?" Jeff asked.

"This sailor don't get rolled, Lieutenant," Zip said. "He's under my protection."

"You couldn't protect a wooden nickel from a blind man. What'd you come looking for, sailor?"

"I told you," Jeff said, annoyed now. "Grandma."

"Tail?"

"Why? You peddling it on the side?"

"Sailor, don't get ..."

"You mean to tell me I could actually find some in this nice, sweet, clean precinct you're so afraid I'm going to foul up?"

"Sailor, I'm talking to you like a friend. Get the hell out of here. Luís, am I giving him bum advice?"

Luís shrugged. "I told him the same thing, Andy!"

"Sure," Parker said, nodding. "Look, Luís lives here. He knows this place like the back of his hand. Did you tell him about this neighborhood, Luís?"

"I told him, I told him."

"About what you run into around here? The guys like Pepe Miranda?"

"*Sí*, ah, there's a one," Luís said.

"What's the matter with Pepe?" Zip asked. "He made you guys look like a bunch of monkeys yesterday." He grinned suddenly. "How many cops did he ambush? Four? Five? Man, he made you look sick." He turned to Jeff. "They walked into the apartment, and in ten seconds he had their guns and was on his his merry way. They're lucky he didn't shoot them, just for kicks."

"Big hero, huh?" Parker said. "He eludes the law, so you make him..."

"I ain't making him nothing. It only seems to me that you big detective masterminds should have got him by now, that's all. Don't you think so?"

"We'll get him," Parker said. "Especially if he came back to this neighborhood."

"*Did* he come back?" Zip asked, leaning forward.

"Maybe," Parker said.

"No kidding?"

Parker shrugged.

"Here? No kidding?"

"You wouldn't happen to know where, would you?"

"Me? Why, Lieutenant, I would tell you instantly if I knew. But, unfortunately, I do not follow the movements of the underworld."

"Luís?" Parker asked, turning to the counter suddenly, as if hoping to catch Luís off guard.

"This is the first I'm hearing, Andy. Why did he come back here? He didn't cause enough trouble here?"

"Who's Pepe Miranda?" Jeff asked.

"Pepe Miranda is a thirty-five-year-old punk. Am I right, Luís?"

"He's only a punk 'cause you can't nab him," Zip said.

"No, no, Andy is right," Luís said. "Miranda's no good. Pghhh, he's rotten."

"Luís and I get along fine," Parker said. "We understand each other. He's been around here as long as I have, and he never so much as spit on the sidewalk." Parker grinned. "He knows I'd drag him down the station house if he did, huh, Luís?"

"Oh, sure, sure," Luís said, riding with the gag.

"Why don't you drag Miranda down the station house, Lieutenant?" Zip asked sweetly.

"Don't think we won't! And cut the lieutenant crap! He's been riding for a fall for a long time now. When a kid has a j.d. card before he's fourteen..."

"A what?" Jeff asked.

"A juvenile delinquency record. At fourteen. So what can you expect? He's no different now than when he started that street gang years ago. The Golden Spaniards. Remember them, Luís? This was even before street gangs were normal around here."

"He was ahead of his time," Zip said, grinning.

"Ahead of his time, my ass."

"No good," Luís said, pulling a face. "I remember. Snotnoses. Like today. No different."

"Except today is the atomic age," Parker said, "so they carry guns instead of knives. Miranda killed a kid in 1942, sailor, when he was seventeen. Slit the kid from ear to ear."

"The kid probably deserved it," Zip said.

"His lawyer got him off with manslaughter," Parker said.

"He should have got the chair," Luís put in. "They should have burned him."

"They sent him upstate, to Castleview, and he spent just enough time there to get out of fighting in World War II. When he was paroled, he came back here. Heroin was the big thing then. Miranda started pushing it."

"Poisoning children! Argh, what makes men do this!"

"Nobody starts on horse unless he wants to, dad," Zip said. "Don't go blaming Miranda."

"Okay by you if we blame him for all the people he's killed in this goddamn city?"

"You can't prove he killed anybody."

"That's what you think. There's a lady dying in General Hospital right now, and she identified a photo of Miranda as the guy who beat her up and took her purse."

"Miranda mugging? Don't snow me, cop."

"Miranda mugging, yes! Not such a goddamn big shot any more, is he? No more high-pay torpedo jobs now that the heat's on. Only little ladies to beat up. Believe me, when we get that bastard we're gonna throw away the key on him."

"Sure, *when* you get him."

"We'll get him. He's here someplace, that's for sure. Once we find out where, goodbye Miranda. One less hero in the neighborhood." He took a long draw at his coffee, finishing it. Putting down the cup, he said, "That was good coffee, Luís. Luís makes the best damn cup of coffee in the city."

"Sure, sure."

"He thinks I'm kidding him. Even if I didn't like you, Luís, I'd still come here to drink your coffee, you know that?"

"It's good having a cop for a steady customer. It keeps trouble away."

"And there's plenty of that around here," Parker said.

"Well, you don't die from being bored around here," Luís said, grinning.

"It's a hell of a lot different from the island, ain't it?"

"Oh, yes, yes."

"I was down there for a week once, had to bring back this punk who skipped the city after holding up a jewelry store on South Fourth. That's the life, all right. Lay in the sun all day long, suck sugar cane, go fishing. And at night..." He winked at Luís. "There's no holding down the Puerto Rican men at night, eh, Luís?"

"Andy, for a man who's a man ... the nights are the same any place, no?"

"Oh, brother, watch out for this guy!" Parker said, laughing. "He's got three kids already, and I think he's gunning for number four."

"At my age?" Luís said, laughing with him. "No, no, it would take a miracle."

"Or a boarder," Parker said. "Keep your eye on the boarder, Luís." He put his hand on Jeff's shoulder. "There are more boarders in this neighborhood than you can shake a stick at. We got areas called 'hot bed' areas, where guys rent out apartments on an eight-hour basis, three sleeping shifts, would you believe it?"

"We don't have any boarders," Luís said, still laughing. "Teresa is safe."

Parker sighed and pulled a handkerchief from his pocket. He wiped his face with it and then said, "Well, back to crime prevention, huh? Sailor, I'd forget that sick grandmother if I was you. Get out of here. This neighborhood ain't for clean-cut kids."

"Who's clean-cut?"

"You're liable to be, if you don't take my advice. From ear to ear, you're liable to be."

"I'll chance it."

"Sure, chance it. Famous last words. I hope you're wearing your dog tags. We'll want to know where to send the body."

"Send it to his grandma," Zip said, grinning. "She's expecting him."

"Kid, you're lucky I'm in a good mood today," Parker said. He turned back to Luís. "Hey, *pinga?*"

"*Sí, cabrón,*" Luís answered, and both men grinned as if pleased by their intimate use of profanity in addressing each other.

"If you hear anything about Miranda, don't forget me, huh?"

"I won't," Luís answered.

"Good. *Adiós.*"

He walked away from the luncheonette, blinking his eyes against the sunshine. He wondered why it was that he could have such a good relationship with Luís Amandez and such a bad one with Frankie Hernandez. Weren't both men Puerto Ricans? Of course they were. But Luís was different. Luís was willing to accept certain things about his own people, whereas Frankie was a son of a bitch who was just deaf and dumb on the subject. How could you hope to discuss anything intelligently with a guy who had a chip on his shoulder? Where was the give and take in a relationship like that? There just wasn't any. Now with Luís, Parker enjoyed a give and take. That's why it was so good. Why couldn't Hernandez be that way, too?

Parker sighed heavily.

It takes all kinds, he told himself. It takes all kinds.

5

Zip continued grinning until Parker had turned the corner and walked off up the avenue. Then the grin dropped from his mouth.

"You'd stool on Pepe for that rotten cop?" he asked Luís.

"Pepe Miranda is no brother of mine," Luís answered.

"A stoolie is a stoolie," Zip said. He swung around and walked to the jukebox. He studied the selections for a moment, inserted his coin, chose one, and then stepped behind the box and turned up the volume so that a mambo fairly blasted into the luncheonette.

"Lower that, lower that," Luís said.

"Shhh, man," Zip said, grinning. "I can't hear the music."

"I said lower that," Luís shouted, and he came around the counter, walked to the juke, and was reaching around to the back when Zip stepped into his way, laughing. The music screeched into the shop, trumpets bellowing, bongo drums pounding their steady beat. At the counter, Jeff's headache responded to the assault wave of sound. He turned toward the juke. The old man was still trying to reach the volume control. Zip, laughing, danced before him, blocking his path, stepping out of it, teasing the old man closer, blocking him again. The grin did not leave his face, but there seemed to be no humor in his laughing defense of the volume control. The old man lunged, and Zip stepped aside finally and danced into the street like a boxer moving away from the ropes. Luís located the volume control and turned it all the way down.

From the street, Zip said, "Not too low, you old bastard. That's still my loot in there."

Luís stamped angrily to the cash register He rang up NO SALE, took a dime from the cash drawer and threw it on the counter. "Here!" he shouted. "Take your money and go!"

Zip threw back his head and laughed, a loud mocking laugh which – like his earlier smile – was totally devoid of humor. "Keep it, dad," he said. "It probably took you all week to make."

"Puncture my eardrums!" Luís muttered. "On a Sunday morning! No decency, no decency!"

But the music, despite Luís' preference fcr comparative silence, seemed to have awakened the neighborhood all at once. The street had been as still and empty as a country road before the record started, and now it suddenly teemed with humanity. In the distance, the church bells had begun tolling again and, in response to the bells, the people of the neighborhood were coming out of the tenements, drifting down the steps leisurely because this was first call, and there was still time before the Mass would begin. The record spun to an end, but the church bells persisted, and the street was alive with color now, color which seemed appropriate to the heat of July, color so vivid, so tropical, that it assailed the eyeballs. Two young girls in the brightest pink came out of a tenement and walked arm in arm down the street toward the church. An old man in a brown silk suit, wearing a bright green tie, came from another tenement and began in the same direction. A woman carrying a red parasol to shield her from the sun walked with the dignity of a queen, trailing a boy in a short-trousered suit by her side. The people nodded at each other, and smiled, and exchanged a few words. This was Sunday morning. This was the day of rest.

From the other end of the street, rushing against the tide of humanity that swelled with a single mind toward the church at the far end of the block, Cooch appeared with two other boys. Zip saw them instantly, and went to join them.

"What the hell kept you so long?" he asked.

"We had to wait for Sixto," Cooch said.

"What the hell are you, Sixto? A man or a baby sitter?"

Sixto looked as if he were about to blush. He was a thin boy of sixteen with eyes that seemed ready to flinch at so much as an unkind word. He spoke English with a Spanish accent which was sometimes marked and sometimes mild. His voice was very soft, and he used it reticently, as if he were not ever certain that anyone wanted to hear what he had to say.

"I ha' to help my mother," he told Zip.

The other boy with Cooch was a six-footer with a face so dark that all personality somehow became lost in the overall impression of blackness. His features were a mixture of Negroid and Caucasian, a mixture so loosely concocted that even here there was an impression of vagueness, of vacuity. The boy was sixteen years old. He moved slowly, and he thought slowly. His mind a blank, his face a blank, he presented a somewhat creaking portrait to his contemporaries, and so they had named him Papá, as befitted a sixteen-year-old who seemed to be seventy.

"When my fodder go on a trip," he said, "I hep my mudder. He tell me to hep her." He spoke with a Spanish accent so marked that sometimes his words were unintelligible. At these moments, he would revert back to his native tongue, and this too added to the concept of a young boy who was old, a young boy who clung to the old language and the old slow-moving ways of a land he had deeply loved.

"That's different," Zip said. "When he's away, you're the man of the house. I'm not talking about a man's work."

Proudly, Papá said, "My fodder's a merchan' marine."

"Who the hell are you snowing?" Zip asked. "He's a waiter."

"On a boat! Tha' makes him a merchan' marine."

"That makes him a waiter! Listen, we've wasted enough time already. Let's lay this out. We're gonna have to move if we want to catch that eleven o'clock Mass." He turned suddenly to Sixto who had been staring blankly at the street. "You with us, Sixto?"

"Wah? Oh, yes. I'm ... I'm with you, Zip."

"You looked like you was on the moon."

"I wass thinkin' ... well, you know. This Alfredo kid, he not sush a bad guy."

"He's getting washed and that's it," Zip said. "I don't even want to hear talk about it." He paused. "What the hell are you looking at, would you please mind telling me?"

"The organ-grinder," Sixto said.

The organ-grinder had rounded the corner and stopped just outside the luncheonette. His parrot had bright-green feathers. The parrot perched on the instrument, accepted coins in his beak, gave them to his master, and then reached down to select a fortune slip from the rack of slips on top of the hand organ. A crowd immediately gathered around the organ-grinder and his trained bird. The crowd was a Sunday churchgoing crowd, bedecked in bright summer colors. The girls shrieked each time they read a fortune. The old men and the old ladies grinned knowingly. Jeff walked out of the luncheonette and handed the parrot a nickel. The parrot reached into the rack, *peck*, a narrow white slip appeared in his beak. Jeff took the slip and began reading it. The girls squealed in delight. There was an innocence surrounding the organ-grinder; the mechanical music he produced was countered by the skill of the bird and the faith of the crowd. For this was Sunday morning, and this was a time to believe in fortunes, a time to believe that the future would be good. And so they crowded the man and his bird, crowded around the sailor who read his fortune from the card and grinned, laughed again in delight as the parrot dipped his beak for another fortune. There was innocence here, and it shimmered on the summer air like truth.

Not ten feet from the organ-grinder, not ten feet from the crowd in their gay Sunday clothes, Zip stood in a whispering circle with three other boys who wore purple silk jackets. The backs of the jackets were lettered with the words THE LATIN PURPLES. The words were cut from yellow felt and stitched to the purple silk. The Latin Purples, The Latin Purples, The Latin Purples, The Latin Purples, four jacket backs and four young men who huddled close together and spoke in low whispers while the organ-grinder filled the air with the music of innocence and truth.

"I ... I wass thinkin'," Sixto said, "maybe we shoul' jus', you know, maybe warn him."

"For messing with one of the debs?" Cooch whispered, astonished.

"So, he dinn really do nothin', Cooch. He jus' ony say hello to her. Thass not so bad."

"He made a grab," Cooch said with finality.

"Thass not what she say. I ask her. She say he ony jus' say hello to her."

"What right did you have to go asking her questions?" Zip wanted to know. "Whose girl is she? Yours or mine?" Sixto remained silent. "Well?"

"Well, Zip," Sixto said, after long deliberation, "I tink ... well, I don' tink she knows. I mean, I don' tink she got no understanding with you."

"I don't need no understanding with a chick. I'm telling you she's my girl, and that's good enough."

"But *she* don' tink so!"

"I don't care what she thinks."

"Anyway," Sixto said, "no matter whose girl she is, if Alfie don' do nothin' to her, why we got to *shoot* him?"

The boys were silent for a moment, as if mention of the word, as if translation of their plan into sound, into a word which immediately delivered the image of a pistol, had shocked them into silence.

In a very low voice, Zip asked, "You going turkey?" Sixto did not answer. "I thought you was a down cat, Sixto. I thought you had heart."

"I *do* got heart."

"He gah heart, Zeep," Papá said, defending Sixto.

"Then why's he backing out? How'd you like it if this was your girl, Sixto? How'd you like it if Alfie went messing around with your girl?"

"But he *dinn* mess with her. He ony say hello. So wha's so bad about dat?"

"You in this club?" Zip asked.

"Sure."

"Why?"

"I ... I don' know. You got to belong to ..." Sixto shrugged. "I don' know."

"If you're in this club, if you wear that purple jacket, you do what I say. Okay. I say the Latin Purples are washing Alfredo Gomez right after eleven o'clock Mass. You want to turkey out, go ahead." He paused meaningfully. "All I know is that Alfie give China a rough time. China's my girl whether she knows it or not, you dig? China's my girl, and that means Alfie got himself trouble."

Cooch nodded. "Big trouble."

"And that don't mean a burn. I don't want him burned. I want him *washed!* You can turkey out, Sixto, go ahead. Only you better watch your step around here afterwards, that's all I'm telling you."

"I jus' thought ... oh, I jus' thought ... well, Zip, cann we *talk* to him?"

"Oh, come on, for Christ's sake!" Zip said angrily.

"Cann we jus' tell him to stop ... to stop talking to her no more? Cann we do dat? Why we have to ... to *kill* him?"

There was another long silence, for another word had been spoken, and this word was stronger than the first. And this word meant exactly what it said, this word meant kill, to take someone's life, kill, to murder. This was not a euphemism, a handy substitute like "wash." This was kill. And the word hung between them, the sentence hung between them on the still July air: "Why we have to ... to *kill* him?"

"Because I say so," Zip said softly.

"It be diff'ren if he really was ..."

"What else you going to do, huh? Get pushed around?" Zip asked. "Man, ain't you sick of all the time getting pushed around?"

"I dinn say that. I said ..."

"Everybody in the neighborhood knows he made a pass at China!" Zip said plaintively. "Am I supposed to ...?"

"He *dinn* make no pass! He ony say hello!"

"Am I supposed to go over and have a chat with him? *How are you, Alfie old boy, how you been? I understand you was feeling up China the other day, was it good?* Am I supposed to hold his goddamn hand, Sixto?"

"No, but ..."

"Don't you want these other clubs to notice us? Don't you want them to know we got self-respect?"

"Sure, but ..."

"So we going to let a creep like Alfie go around screwing our debs?"

Sixto shook his head. "Zip, Zip, he dinn even..."

"Okay, listen to me," Zip said. "After we pull this today, we're in. You understand that? We wash this creep, and there ain't nobody in this neighborhood who don't know the Latin Purples from then on in. They'll know we don't get pushed around by *anybody!* Every damn kid on this block'll want to be in the club after today. We're gonna be... something! *Something!*" He paused to catch his breath. His eyes were glowing. "Am I right, Cooch?"

"Sure," Cooch answered.

"Okay, Alfie's going to eleven o'clock Mass, like he always does. Mass'll break around eleven-forty, a quarter to twelve. I want to get him on the steps as he's coming out."

"On dee—!"

"*On the steps!* All four of us blast together, and nobody stops until Alfie's down. You better shoot straight 'cause there'll be a lot of innocent people around."

"Zip, on dee church steps?" Sixto said. His face was twisted in pain. "*Ave Maria,* cann we...?"

"On the steps, I said! Where everybody'll see him die. We've got four pieces. I'm using the .45 because I want to blow that creep's head off."

The organ-grinder stopped his music. The street seemed suddenly silent.

"There's two .38s and the Luger," Zip whispered. "Take whatever you want."

"The Luger," Cooch said.

"You got it. Sixto, you and Papá'll use the .38s. The pieces are up at my pad. We get them first, and then round up a couple of gun bearers." He paused for a moment. "Second thought, you better stay here, Sixto. Keep an eye on Alfie's house. Right around the corner. The first building."

"Okay," Sixto said blankly.

"Make sure he don't leave. If he does, follow him. If you ain't here when we get back, we'll start looking for you."

"Okay."

"What?"

"I said okay."

'Okay," Zip repeated. "Come on." He put his arm around Cooch as they began walking toward his building, Papá shuffling along beside them. "You excited, Cooch?" he asked.

"Huh? Oh, yeah, I guess. A little."

"Man, I'm excited. This day is beginning to tick, you know what I mean? Things are moving!"

"Yeah, that's true," Cooch said.

"Some Sundays, you can sit on that front stoop and go nuts. Especially like now in the summer. But today is different. Today, there's like a million things to do, ain't there? What I'm trying to say, Cooch, this makes me feel good. This action, you know? Man, it makes me feel real good!"

Cooch grinned as the three boys entered the tenement. "It ain't gonna make Alfie feel so good," he said.

Sixto stood on the corner outside the luncheonette, watching Alfredo's building, nervously biting his lower lip.

Inside the luncheonette, Jeff handed his fortune slip to Luís and said, "How do you like that?"

"Be patient and of firm resolve," Luís read, "and you will achieve all your ends."

"Yeah," Jeff said. "What time does La Gallina open?"

"I had hoped you would forget La Gallina."

"Well, since I'm already up here..." Jeff shrugged and let the sentence trail. "What time does it open?"

"This is Sunday," Luís said, "and La Gallina is a bar – among other things. It does not open until noon."

"Then I've got plenty of time yet."

"If you'd take my advice..."

"*Hey! Hey you!*" the voice bellowed, and they both turned simultaneously to face the street. Andy Parker seemed to have materialized from nowhere. He approached Sixto, who stood on the corner, and shouted, "*You! You there!*"

Sixto, frightened, began to inch away from him "Me?" he asked. "Me?"

"What are you doing?" Parker asked, coming up close to him.

"Nothin'. I wass ony jus' standin'..."

"Against the wall!"

"Huh?"

Parker seized his jacket front and slammed him up against the supporting post at the corner of the luncheonette. "I said against the wall!"

"I ... I dinn do nothin'," Sixto said. "I wass only jus'..."

"Bend over!"

Sixto stared at him blankly, uncomprehendingly.

"Bend over, goddamnit!" Parker shouted.

Sixto still did not understand. Furiously, because he felt his command was being openly flouted, Parker chopped a fast right to Sixto's gut, doubling him over. He spun him around then so that he faced the corner post, his hands clutching his stomach, his head bent.

"Put your hands against the wall, palms flat, goddamnit, do what I tell you!" Parker shouted.

Sixto, doubled over with pain, made an abortive attempt to stretch out his arms, clutched his stomach again, and then shoved his arms out convulsively when Parker hit him in the ribs. He extended his hands and placed them, trembling, against the corner post. Quickly, Parker frisked him. He did an intent and thorough job, so thorough that he did not notice Frankie Hernandez who walked up the street and stopped just short of the luncheonette.

"Turn around!" Parker shouted. "Now empty your pockets! Everything on the sidewalk! Hurry up!"

Hernandez walked to where they were standing. "Leave him alone, Andy," he said. He turned to Sixto. "Take off, kid."

Sixto hesitated, frightened, looking first to one detective and then the other.

"Get out of here, go ahead! Beat it!"

Sixto hesitated a moment longer, and then broke into a sprint around the corner, racing up the avenue.

"Thanks, Frankie," Parker said sarcastically.

"There's nothing in the penal code that makes it a crime for a kid to be minding his own business, Andy."

"Who's saying anything?" Parker said. He paused. "But suppose that nice innocent kid was holding a deck of heroin?"

"He wasn't holding anything. He's no junkie, and you know it. He comes from a good family."

"Oh, is that right? Junkies don't come from good families, huh? Suppose he *was* holding, Frankie? Just suppose?"

"The only thing he's holding right now is contempt for the cop who shook him down."

"Seems to me you should be interested in looking up the people who are doing something wrong," Jeff said from the luncheonette.

"We do, sailor," Parker answered. "Day and night. That kid belongs to a street gang, don't he? You saw his club jacket, didn't you? Do you expect me to take crap from every hoodlum on the street?"

"That kid probably has little enough self-respect as it is," Hernandez said. "So you come along and . . ."

"All right, all right, cut it out with the kid, will you? Boy, you'd think I worked him over with a rubber hose." He paused. "Where you headed?"

"To see the Gomez woman," Hernandez said.

"She was quite a little trick, that Gomez woman. Pushing fifty, maybe, but still got it all in the right places. You sure this is a business call, Frankie?"

"I'm sure," Hernandez said.

"Well, just so long as you're sure. Was there any word on Miranda back at the squad?"

"Not when I left, no."

"You know," Luís said thoughtfully, "I think maybe Frankie's right. I don't mean to tell you how to do your job, Andy. Don't think that. But this boy could be hurt by such treatment. What I mean ... well ... on the island, it was not this way."

"Juvenile gangs ain't a problem in Puerto Rico," Parker said flatly.

"No, of course not, but that's not what I meant. There just seemed to be ... I don't know ... more respect there."

"For what? For siestas?" Parker asked, and he burst out laughing.

"Well, now you're making it a joke," Luís said, embarrassed.

"Me? Why should I joke about your homeland?"

"It was just ... you know ... we were poor and hungry, true. But there was always the plaza in the center of town, and the pink church, and the poinsettias, and the mango trees. And you could go to the plaza and talk to your friends. And you were a person, and people knew your name. It was important, Andy. You knew who you were."

"Who were *you*, Luís?" Parker said, chuckling. "The governor?"

"Ah, he makes it a joke," Luís said good-naturedly. "*You* know what I mean, don't you, Frankie?"

"Yes. I know what you mean."

"Sometimes here, you feel lost. And without identity, there can be no dignity, no respect."

"I know just what you mean, Louise," Jeff said. "It's like what I was telling you about Fletcher. How you can just get swallowed up in a pile of people and forget who and what you are."

"*Sí, sí*. The island had respect for people, and for life ... and respect for death, too. Life is cheap here, and death is cheaper. On the island..." He paused, as if giving himself time for the memory to grow, to blossom in his mind. "On the island," he said, "in the towns, when there is a funeral, the casket bearers walk in the center of the main street, and the mourners follow behind the casket."

"I know this," Hernandez said softly. "My father used to talk about this."

"About the little girls dressed in white, carrying their flowers in the sunshine?" Luís said. "The town all dusty and quiet and still."

"Yes," Hernandez said. "About that."

"And the shopkeepers stand in their doorways, and when the casket goes by, they close the doors. They are showing respect for the dead man. They are saying, 'I will not conduct business while you pass by, my friend.'"

"Argh, bullshit," Parker said. "That ain't respect. They're just scared of death. I'll tell you something, Luís. I don't know what it's like on that island of yours, but here — right *here* — the only ones who get respect are the live ones — the hoodlums like Pepe Miranda."

Luís shook his head quickly and emphatically. "No," he said.

"No, huh? Take my word for it."

"I'm going," Hernandez said. "You argue it out between you."

"Who's arguing?" Parker said. "We're having a discussion."

"Okay, so discuss it," Hernandez said, and he walked out of the luncheonette and around the corner.

Jeff swung around on his stool and stared up the street. Behind him, he could hear the detective and Luís arguing — well, discussing — but he was not interested in what they were saying. He kept staring at the closed door of La Gallina, wondering when the bar would open. He really didn't know whether he actually felt like spending the day in bed with a woman or not, but he couldn't think of much else to do with his time. And he *had* come all the way uptown, and he hated to think of the trip as a total loss. So he kept staring at the closed door, almost willing it to open and – quite miraculously – it opened.

6

The girl who stepped out of the bar was no more than nineteen years old, a slender girl with the curved body of a woman thrusting against the sweater and skirt she wore. Her hair was black, and her eyes were dark. She took a key from her purse and was leaning over to lock the door when Jeff got off his stool and ran up the street.

"Hi," he said.

The girl whirled, surprised. Her eyes opened wide, the brownest eyes Jeff had ever seen in his entire life.

"Oh!" she said, and her lips rounded over the single word, and slowly the shock gave way to puzzlement, and she stared at him curiously, waiting for him to speak.

"I've been waiting for you all morning," Jeff said. "Were you in there all along?"

"Yes?" she said, delivering the word as a question, as if she expected further explanation from him and was waiting for it. He continued to watch her. A slow realization was coming to him. He was beginning to recognize the fact that this was possibly the most beautiful girl he'd ever met, and her beauty left him somewhat tongue-tied. The girl waited. Jeff remained speechless. Finally, she tucked the key into her purse, gave a small feminine shrug, and began walking away. Jeff stepped around her quickly, directly into her path.

"Hey, where you going?" he said.

"Home."

"Why? I only just found you."

"I have to get dressed," the girl said.

"You look dressed fine to me," he said, and his eyes traveled the length of her body, pausing on the soft swell of her breasts beneath the light-blue sweater, the abrupt curve of her hips against the black skirt.

"I have to get dressed," the girl repeated blankly, seemingly embarrassed by his scrutiny.

"Well, that can wait, can't it?" he asked.

The girl seemed very puzzled. "What do you want?" she said.

"Well ... uh ... don't *you* know?"

"No?" the girl said, and again she raised her voice at the end of the word so that it sounded like a question.

"Well ... I was talking to a fellow last night. It was really very early this morning. Downtown. In a bar."

"Yes?"

"And he said I should come up here."

"What for?"

"He said I'd find you here," Jeff said.

He looked at her, and he thought, Well, he didn't exactly say I would find you here, because no one ever expects to find something like you, no one ever really expects to come across something like you ever in his life.

"He didn't say that," the girl said.

"Yes. Yes, he did."

"What was his name? The man who told you about me?"

"I don't remember," Jeff paused. "I was drunk."

"Are you drunk now?"

He smiled tentatively. "Sober as a judge."

"And this fellow told you about *me?* He said you would find *me?*"

"Well ... not exactly. I mean, I didn't expect anyone as ... as pretty as you. But he said—"

"What *did* he say, exactly?"

"He said I should go uptown..."

"Yes?"

"And I should look for a place called La Gallina."

"La Ga— oh." She paused and looked at him more closely. "I see. Yes. Now I understand."

"Good. I got to admit, you're really something. I mean a guy just doesn't expect ... I mean, I'm not trying to say anything against what you do, or anything like that ... but ... well, you know, it's just unusual, that's all. To find one as pretty as you."

"Thank you," the girl said. She smiled. "I think you've made a mistake."

"This *is* La Gallina, isn't it?" Jeff asked, looking at the gilt lettering on the plate-glass windows again.

"Oh, yes. This is La Gallina."

"And you did come out of there, didn't you?"

"Yes, I certainly did."

There was a strange twinkle in her brown eyes. He looked at her suspiciously and realized she was trying to suppress a laugh.

"You *do* work in there?" he asked. "Don't you?"

"I do."

"Well, what's so funny?" he said, beginning to get slightly annoyed.

The girl would not allow the laugh to escape her mouth. "Nothing," she said. "Nothing."

"Well, then, all right," he said.

"All right," she answered.

They stood staring at each other, Jeff trying to figure out

what was so goddamned funny, and the girl trying her best not to laugh.

"Well?" he said at last.

"Well what?"

"Well, let's go to bed."

"You and me?"

"Well, sure, you and me. Who did you think I meant?"

The girl shook her head. "No. I don't think so."

She started to move away from him, and he caught her arm, stopping her.

"Why not?"

"Well ..." Again, she held back a laugh. She thought for a moment, and then said, "I guess I don't like sailors."

"That's no attitude," Jeff said, grinning. "Some of my best friends are sailors."

"No," the girl said, shaking her head. "No. Sorry. No sailors." She saw the disappointment on his face and quickly added, "Besides, I'm too high."

"High?"

"Yes, my price. My ... uh ... my fee?" She made it sound as if she were asking him what the correct word should be.

"Well, how high is high?" Jeff asked, beginning to bargain.

"A lot." The girl considered the question gravely. "More than you earn in a week."

"How much is that?"

"Very, very high," she said.

"Well, how much? Can't you tell me? Boy, you sure act strange for a ..."

"I told you," the girl said. "Very very very high." She seemed at a loss for words. She struggled with her thoughts and then desperately said, "What's the highest you ever paid?"

"Twenty. But that was on the Coast. On the Coast ..."

"I'm much higher than that," she said quickly, seemingly relieved.

"Forty?"

"Higher."

"A hundred?" he asked, appalled.

"Goodness," the girl said, her eyes twinkling again. "Do I look like a common streetwalker?"

"Well, no, no," he said hastily, "you don't. But a hundred dollars, God, I..."

"I didn't say a hundred. I said higher."

"I haven't even got twenty," he said despondently. "You see, I was in a poker game and..."

"Well, there are other girls," she said curtly. "Goodbye."

She turned on her heel and began walking up the street. Jeff watched her and then, galvanized into sudden action, he yelled, "Hey! Wait!" and ran after her.

"What is it?" she said.

"Listen, can't we talk this over?"

"Why?"

"Well, I ... I think you're pretty."

"Thank you."

"I mean it. I'm not just saying it so you'll..." He paused. "I mean it."

"Why don't you go home, sailor?" she said kindly, her face suddenly turning so tender that he wanted to kiss her right then and there in the street, even though you weren't supposed to kiss girls like this, still he wanted—

"Home?" he said. "Hell, I live in Colorado. Listen, can't we talk this over?"

"Sailor—"

"Jeff."

"Jeff, all right, Jeff, I'm not what you think. I'm not what the fellow sent you uptown for."

"Huh?"

"I cook for La Gallina and some of the other bars. They have steam tables. I prepare the food for them."

"You pre— oh." He paused. "So you were in there..."

"Getting things ready for when they open," the girl said, nodding.

"Oh." He paused again. "And all that business about price ..."

"I was fooling you."

"Oh. Well, I'm sorry."

"That's all right. I'm sorry I fooled you."

"Oh, that's all right." He studied her soberly. "You're still very pretty."

"Thank you."

"Do you ... do you have to run off?"

"I have to get dressed. I'm going to church."

"I'll go with you," he said quickly.

"Are you Catholic?"

"Presbyterian. I'll go with you anyway. I've gone to all kinds of religious services in the Navy. I'm something of an expert. You see, I do it to get out of work parties. Whenever I'm on a work party and they announce like, 'All people of the Jewish faith, prepare to leave the ship for religious services,' I all of a sudden become a person of the Jewish faith. I'm just sorry there aren't less work parties and more religions."

The girl shook her head. "I would feel funny."

"Are you religious? Is that it?"

"I suppose so. Yes."

"Well, I mean, the church won't fall down or anything if I walk into it. Believe me. I've been inside Catholic churches before. It's a nice service." He nodded, thinking over the various services he had been to.

"I would still feel funny," the girl said. She looked at him in indecision, and then made a slight movement of departure.

"Look," he said. "Look ... don't run off."

"Why not?"

"I don't know."

"You'll be busy," she said. "La Gallina opens at noon."

"Well, that ... you know, it's not that important."

"Isn't it?"

"No, it isn't," he said firmly. "Look, won't you ... won't you stay with me?"

The girl looked at her watch. "I have to go," she said. "I want to catch the eleven o'clock Mass."

"Will you meet me after church?"

"Why should I?"

"I want you to. Don't you want to?"

The girl hesitated. Then she said, "Yes, I do."

"Then why don't you?"

"Are you on a ship?"

"Yes. Look, will you ..."

"What kind?"

"A destroyer."

"Is it big?"

"Pretty big. Will you meet me?"

"Why do you want to meet me? Haven't you got a girl back home?"

"I used to, but not any more. Have ... have you got a ... a boy?"

"No."

"Good. That's good." He smiled.

"Yes," she said, and she returned the smile.

"Will you ... will you meet me?"

"If I do ... would we go someplace outside the neighborhood?"

"If you like."

"Where will we go?"

"I don't know. I don't know this city too well."

"But we will leave the neighborhood?"

"Yes. You see, if we were back in Colorado, I'd take you up in the mountains. We'd pack a picnic basket and go up in the mountains. I'd drive you in my car. I've got a '37 Ford."

"What color is it?"

"Yellow. I painted it myself."

"I knew it was yellow," she said.

"Did you? How'd you know?"

"Yellow or red. Those are the two colors I thought."

"Hey, you know I *was* going to paint it red but Jenken's – that's the hardware store back home – was all out. So I took yellow."

"Do you live in a very small town?"

"Fletcher? Well, it's not *so* small, you understand."

"Do you have apartment buildings?"

"Oh, no."

"Why did you leave home?"

"I wanted to see the world," he said glibly, and then he knew immediately that glibness was not for this girl. With this girl you played it straight or you didn't play it at all. "I was going to get drafted," he said, "so I figured I'd rather be in the Navy. So I enlisted." He shrugged.

"And the world? Have you seen it?"

"A little of it."

"Have you been to Puerto Rico?"

"No. Have you?"

"No. It's supposed to be beautiful there. I was born here. I've never been outside this city." She paused. "Oh, yes, I once went to a wedding in Pennsylvania."

"You'd like my town," he said. "You really would."

"Yes, I know I would."

They fell silent. She stared up at him, and he felt terribly unsure of himself all at once, unsure and far younger than he actually was. In a very small voice, he said, "Meet me after church. Please."

"If I met you, we could go to the park," she said. "There are no mountains, but we could take a picnic basket. There are trees there."

"Any place you say. Only ... you know ... I've only got about eighteen bucks. We can go as far as that'll take us." He grinned tentatively. "Okay?"

The girl nodded. "Okay."

"Gee, that's— You'll meet me?"

"Yes."

"Look, I'll ... I'll meet you right here. Right on this spot. I won't budge from this spot until you come back."

"No, not here. When La Gallina opens, the girls'll congregate here, on the sidewalk. Not here."

"The luncheonette then, okay? On the corner."

"Luís? All right, fine."

"What time?"

"Mass'll be over at about a quarter to twelve. I'll make the lunch now and—"

"Hey, you don't have to—"

"I want to."

"Well ... okay."

"And I'll stop home for it before I come. Twelve o'clock? Would that be all right?"

"Fine. Hey, listen, I'm sorry I mistook you for ..."

"That's all right. Twelve?"

"Twelve," he said.

"All right." She stared at him for a moment and then said, "Wait for me."

"Yes, I will."

She turned and began walking up the street, walking quickly, not looking back, almost as if she knew his eyes were on her, almost as if she were waiting for him to call after her. When he did call, she whirled immediately.

"Hey!"

"Yes?"

"Hurry! Please hurry, would you?"

"Yes," she said. She gave a small wave, turned, and began walking again.

"Hey!" he called.

"Yes?"

"I don't even know your name!"

"What?"

"Your name," he shouted. "What's your name?"

"Oh," the girl said, and she giggled.

"Well, what is it?"

"China!" she called back, and then she ran up the street.

7

Heat is a strange thing.

Like love, it can drive men to opposite extremes. Like love, it can be a persistently nagging thing, relentless, unwilling to budge, until one day it explodes in wild passion. "I hit him with the hatchet because it was hot." That is an explanation, a reason, and an excuse. It was hot. Everything is contained in those three words. It was hot, and so I was not responsible for my actions, I only knew that it was hot, that I was suffocating all day long, that I could hardly breathe, there was no air, it was hot, and he said to me, "This coffee is too strong," and so I hit him with the hatchet. It was hot, you see.

A shrug.

You understand. It was hot.

And, like love, the heat can generate a different kind of feeling, a feeling which – had the slick paper magazines not defiled the word – could be described as togetherness, a knowledge that human beings on this day, on this insufferably hot day, are at least sharing one thing in common. The heat becomes a bond as strong as reinforced concrete. Do you hate the color of my skin? That is interesting, but God it is hot, God we are sweating together. Do you lech for my wife? That is unforgivable, but let's go have a beer together to escape this damned heat, and later we can work it out.

Heat, like love, is no good unless you can talk about it. The adulterer seeks a confidante, the lecher boasts of his conquests in the pool hall, the sixteen-year-old cheerleader spends hours on the telephone describing a football player's kiss – you have to talk about love.

Lieutenant Peter Byrnes came out of his office wanting to talk about the heat. He was a compact man with graying hair and steel-blue eyes. He liked to believe that he sweated more than men who were less chunky than he. He liked to believe that the heat had been designed in hell especially for him, sent earthward to plague him. He didn't quite understand why he'd been singled out for such torture, but he did know that he suffered more when it was hot than any man had a right to suffer.

The squadroom was silent. Steve Carella, his shirt sleeves rolled up, was sitting at his desk, reading an FBI report on a suspected burglar. Hot sunlight covered the top of his desk like molasses. Byrnes walked to the grilled window and stared out at the street. The cars, the people, all seemed to have been captured in transparent plastic, suspended in time and space, unmoving. Byrnes sighed.

"Hot," he said.

"Mmm," Carella answered.

"Where is everybody?"

"Parker's on the prowl, Hernandez is answering a squeal, and Kling..." Carella shrugged. "He's on a plant, isn't he?"

"That drugstore thing?"

"I think so."

"Yeah," Byrnes said, remembering. "The guy who's passing

phony cocaine prescriptions." He shook his head. "He won't turn up. Not in this heat."

"Maybe not," Carella said.

"I always choose the wrong time for my vacation," Byrnes said. "Harriet and I spend months figuring it out. I'm the senior officer around here, so I get first choice. So what happens? I always miss the good weather by a month. It's so hot you can't even think, and then it's time for my vacation, and it starts raining, or it turns gray, or we suddenly get a snowstorm from Canada. It never fails. Every year." He paused for a moment. "Well, every year except one. We went to the Vineyard once. We had good weather." He nodded, remembering.

"Vacations are rough anyway," Carella said.

"Yeah? How so?"

"I don't know. It generally takes me two weeks to unwind, and the minute I start relaxing, it's time to come back to work."

"You going away this year?"

"I don't think so. The kids are too small."

"How old are they, anyway?" Byrnes asked.

"They were a year old in June."

"Boy, time flies," Byrnes said, and fell silent. He thought about the passage of time, thought about his own son, thought how much Carella seemed like a son to him, thought how his squadroom seemed like a family business, a candy store or a grocery store, thought how good it was to have Carella working behind the counter with him.

"Well, talking about the heat never helped it any," Byrnes said, and he sighed again.

"Some day, they're going to invent..." Carella started, and the telephone rang. He picked up the receiver. "Eighty-seventh Squad," he said. "Detective Carella."

The voice on the other end said, "I know where Pepe Miranda iss."

*   *   *

They saw Sixto as he came out of the drugstore. His face looked flushed. It seemed as if he were about to cry. He kept blinking his eyes like a person fighting to hold back tears.

"What's the matter?" Zip asked. He studied Sixto impersonally, not as if he were truly concerned, not as if he really wanted to know what the matter was, but asking the disguised question, "How will your present state affect *me*?"

"Nothin'," Sixto said.

"You look like somebody hit you with a ball bat."

"No."

"What were you doing in the drugstore?"

"Havin' a Coke. I wass thirsty."

"I thought I told you to keep an eye on Alfie's pad."

"I could see his buildin' from where I wass sittin'," Sixto said.

"We gah dee guns," Papá said, grinning.

"Come on," Zip told them both. "Cooch is rounding up some kids. We got to meet him near the luncheonette."

They walked down the avenue together, Zip in the middle flanked by Sixto and Papá. He felt rather good with the boys on either side of him. He walked with his shoulders back and his head erect, setting the pace, knowing they would keep up with him, and feeling very friendly towards the boys as he walked, feeling a bond with them which he could not have described accurately if he'd tried. There was no logic to the bond because he admitted to himself that he didn't even particularly like either Sixto or Papá. One was a mama's boy and the other was a half-wit. And yet he could not deny the emotional satisfaction of walking down the avenue with these two by his side, like a general with his trusted aides. The bond, he knew, would become stronger once they had washed Alfredo Gomez. The word crossed his mind, washed, and he was instantly face to face with the other word, the stronger word. Kill. He did not flinch from it. Kill. He repeated the word in his mind. Kill. We will kill Alfredo Gomez. Kill.

By the time they reached the luncheonette, the word had
no more meaning to him than the word "wash". Cooch was
there, waiting for them. Two small boys were with him.
Parker, the bull, had taken off, but the sailor was still
inside the luncheonette, probably waiting for La Gallina to
open, waiting for a Spanish girl. The idea pleased Zip at
first. He felt a fierce pride in the knowledge that the sailor
had come uptown to seek the passion only a Spanish girl
could give him. And then the pride turned sour, and he
thought darkly that the sailor had no right to be here, no
right to be emptying himself into Spanish girls, the way
sewers empty into the river. He frowned and cast a black
scowl at the sailor's back, and then walked quickly to where
Cooch stood with the younger boys.

The first of the boys was wearing dungarees and a white,
sweat-stained T shirt. His nose was running, and he constantly wiped at it with the back of his hand, the mucus
streaked there like a healed burn. He was eight years old.

The other boy was nine. He wore khaki shorts and a
short-sleeved blue sports shirt. An Army sergeant's stripes
had been sewn to the left sleeve of the shirt. He moved his feet
constantly, as if trying to erase chalk from the sidewalk.

"These the kids?" Zip asked Cooch.

"Yeah," Cooch said.

Zip looked at the one with the snotty nose. "What's your
name, kid?"

"Chico."

"And yours?" he said to the other boy.

"Estaban," the boy answered, his feet erasing invisible
chalk.

"Did Cooch explain the picture to you?"

"*Sí*," Chico said.

"You and Estaban, one on each side of the church steps.
You keep the pieces under your shirts until we get on the
scene. Then you give them to us and hang around until

we blast. We give you back the pieces when it's all over, and you cut out. You got that?"

"*Sí, yo comprendo,*" Chico said.

"*Sí, sí,*" Estaban echoed, his feet moving nervously. He seemed undecided as to whether he should break into a dance or begin stamping the sidewalk in anger. Nervously, his feet continued moving.

Zip looked at his watch. "Okay, the church bells should begin ringing any minute now. That'll be first call for the eleven o'clock Mass. You kids cut out as soon as you hear them bells. We'll drift up toward the corner around eleven-thirty. You be ready for us, you hear me?"

"Zip, when we grow up, me an' Estaban," Chico said, "we coul' go gang-bustin' wi' you?"

Zip grinned and touched the boy's hair. "Sure, when you grow up. Right now, you have them pieces ready for us when we need them."

"I know how to shoot, Zip," Chico said. "I know how to shoot good."

Zip laughed aloud. "Not this trip, Chico. You got time yet before you begin..."

The church bells rang suddenly, abruptly, and then were silent. Whoever was pulling on the cord had made an abortive start, perhaps the cord had slipped from his hands, perhaps he'd had a sudden cramp in his fingers. The heavy solemn bonnnnng of metal upon metal sounded, reverberated, and then died. The boys stood in silence, straining for the peal of the bells. And then the bells started again, ringing out on the still July air, calling the flock to Mass, reaching into the streets and into the open windows, summoning the congregation, summoning Alfredo Gomez to whatever waited for him on the church steps.

"That's it," Zip said tightly. He reached beneath his jacket and, one by one, began pulling the weapons from where they were tucked into his belt. Jeff, in the luncheonette, turned at the sound of the church bells, thinking of China, a smile on his face. He saw the first weapon pass from Zip's hand to Chico's snot-smeared fist, and he blinked as the other weapons changed hands, watched as the two youngsters tucked them into their waistbands, four guns in all, and then pulled their shirts down over them.

"Okay, go," Zip said.

The two boys grinned, nodded, and then ran off up the street. A frown had come onto Jeff's forehead. He swung his stool around and picked up his cup of coffee. The church bells had stopped now. An old man rushed from the mouth of a tenement, paused on the stoop while he pulled on his suit jacket, and then ran spryly up the street.

"Nice quiet Sunday," Luís said to Jeff, smiling.

Jeff nodded and said nothing. The four boys in the purple silk jackets had moved to a position near the jukebox. The street had gone silent again. It seemed to be a street of many moods and many temperaments, changing in the space of seconds like a vaudeville performer who snaps a wig into place and becomes a clown, discards the wig, puts on a black mustache and becomes Adolf Hitler. Now, the street in its sunbath seemed like a golden corridor leading to the high overhead arch of the elevated structure two blocks away, the sky a dazzling yellow-white beyond. Quiet, burning with light, the street was mute, the street waited. The boys lounged near the jukebox, their hands in their pockets. Occasionally they glanced in the direction of the church. Their eyes were squinted against the reflected sunlight.

The girl turned the corner from the avenue and entered the street like a circus train. She was wearing a bright-red jacket, a bright-yellow silk shirt, purple spiked-heel shoes with ankle straps. Her hair was a mass of thick black, sticking out from her head in near-burlesque of a Bushman. She was carrying a bright-blue carpetbag, and she walked with a suggestive swagger, the yellow skirt tightening over plump, jiggling buttocks, huge breasts jutting from the V-necked opening of the red jacket. She seemed to be wearing nothing under her outer clothing, and she didn't give a damn who realized it. Her buttocks begged to be pinched, her breasts beneath the white rayon blouse and the red jacket pointed sharp nipples like compass needles indicating north. Her walk did nothing to hide the pulchritude. This was what she owned, and if she preferred to exhibit her possessions, that was her business.

But despite the suggestive swagger, despite the bobbing breasts and the fluid grinding motion of buttock against buttock, despite an apparent attitude of indifference, the girl seemed frightened and somehow hesitant. She stared up at the buildings, ogling the city, overwhelmed by the size, somewhat confused and a little lost.

The whistles that came from Zip and Cooch did not help her at all. She suddenly clutched at the small red jacket in an attempt to close it over her thrusting breasts. The boys whistled again, and Jeff turned to watch the girl, fascinated by the tautness of the yellow skirt and the bobble of her backside. The girl began walking faster, just as lost, just as confused, and the whistles followed her up the street until she was out of sight.

Zip began laughing.

And then his laughter stopped when he realized the sailor was laughing too.

"What was *that*?" Jeff asked.

"Argh, a Marine Tiger," Luís said.

"A what?"

"Marine Tiger. Fresh from the island, her first day here probably. Marine Tiger. That was the name of one of the first boats to take Puerto Rican immigrants to the mainland."

"Boy, that was really something," Jeff said.

"Did you see that hair?" Luís waved his hands around his head in demonstration. "And now she'll ride the subway, and everyone will think all Puerto Ricans are like her." He shook his head. "I need more soup out here," he said vaguely and went into the back of the shop.

"I wouldn't have minded dumping her on her back, huh, sailor?" Zip said.

"Well, she's not exactly my type," Jeff said. He turned back to the counter. He did not like talking to this boy, and he did not wish to encourage a friendship which, now that he was sober and now that he had met China, seemed hardly necessary.

"Not your type, huh?" Zip said. "What's the matter? You don't like Spanish girls?"

"I didn't say that."

Zip lighted a cigarette and blew out a stream of smoke. He considered his next words carefully. He did not know why, but the sailor was beginning to annoy him immensely. At one and the same time, he wanted the sailor to desire a Spanish girl, and yet wanted him to have nothing to do with a Spanish girl. The conflict disturbed him. He frowned as he began speaking.

"I've got a few minutes to kill. You still interested in a girl, I can fix you up with something real nice."

"I'm not interested," Jeff said.

"No?" The frown got deeper. "Why not? You got something against Puerto Rican girls?"

"No. I'm just not interested any more."

"What'd you come up here for? A girl, right?"

"That's right," Jeff said.

His answer angered Zip. "So why won't you let me get you one?"

"I told you. I'm not interested any more."

"Then why are you hanging around here?"

"That's my business," Jeff said curtly.

"If you ain't interested any more, why don't you get out of the neighborhood?"

"You ask a lot of questions," Jeff said.

"Yeah, that's right. What about it?"

"Suppose you answer one," Jeff said.

"I don't have to an—"

"Why'd you pass out those guns?"

Zip's eyes opened wide. "What?"

"You handed an arsenal to those two kids. Who do you plan on shooting?"

They sat side by side on adjacents stools, Jeff's fists bunched on the counter, Zip's eyes narrowing as the sailor's words penetrated. The other boys, with the exception of Sixto, had moved away from the jukebox, and advanced towards their leader.

"You got big eyes, Grandma," Zip said, as he suddenly struck Jeff full in the face with his closed fist. Jeff, surprised by the blow, tried to maintain his balance on the stool, realized intuitively that it would be a mistake to fall, a mistake to be on the ground. He clutched for the counter top, but the imbalance was complete and his hand slid over the Formica top as he went over and back, his foot hooked into the stool's rung, the asphalt tile floor coming up to meet his back. He caught the force of the fall with his shoulder blades, snapping his head so that it wouldn't collide with the floor. He was struggling to get his foot free of the rung when the first kick exploded against the side of his head.

He brought up his hands instinctively, trying to free his foot, squirming to get his foot loose from this ridiculously foolish position, and the second kick caught him in the rib cage, and he felt all the breath in his body escape from his mouth in a grunt, and then another kick caught the side of his neck, and now the kicks were coming with methodical precision and his foot was still hooked into that goddamn rung, a boot connected with his right eye and he felt shocking, stabbing pain and then the warmth of blood and he thought I'm going to be kicked to death on the floor of this goddamn luncheonette and then he heard Luis shouting, "What are you doing? Bastards, what are you doing?" And above that, or beyond it, around it, circling it, filling the air, the high penetrating wail of a police siren.

8

Hernandez had seen this apartment before, had been inside it. Not this one, exactly, but countless others like it in buildings of the precinct. This could have been the very apartment he had lived in as a boy.

The front door opened into the kitchen. There was the usual police lock; the first plate screwed to the door, the second plate embedded in the floor, and the unbending steel bar which, when wedged into its triangular place between the two, made forcible entry impossible. A window was at the far end of the kitchen. It opened on the interior shaftway of the tenement. There was linoleum on the kitchen floor, a spatter pattern. It had been scrubbed clean but left unwaxed. It had worn through in patches near the door, the icebox, and the stove. A white enamel-topped table was on the wall opposite the stove. A picture of Jesus in supplication was above the table. The walls were painted a pale green, but the grime of countless meals in preparation had worn itself into the walls so that the green seemed darker, bile-like. The paint, too, was beginning to flake off in several places on the walls and on the ceiling. A toaster was on the table. A plastic shield covered it. The room seemed shoddy but clean. It was a room he remembered well.

On winter days, when he was a boy, he would sit on the floor by the stove, playing with his soldiers on the clean worn linoleum. His mother had miraculously managed to cook her meals with him underfoot. The smells of *arroz con pollo* would fill the kitchen, and it was cozy by the stove where he endowed each of his metal men with a personality and an identity. There was warmth in the kitchen of the Hernandez home, warmth from the stove and the smell of cooking food, warmth in the gentle voice of his mother as she went about her work, warmth in the monologues the boy Frankie addressed to the metal men surrounding him.

There was no warmth in the Gomez kitchen on that day in July, no warmth but the suffocating heat of summer. Outside, they could hear the wail of the siren. Mrs. Gomez went to the window and closed it. The sound withdrew.

"Always fires," she said. "Always the sirens. Never a day without a fire." She shook her head. "And it's worse in the winter."

"Where's the boy?" Hernandez asked.

"In the bedroom. Frankie, please go easy with him. This thing he is in, it is great trouble. But ... he is hard to know."

"I'll go easy," Hernandez said.

She led him through the apartment, into the "parlor" furnished with a three-piece living-room suite, a television set, a floor lamp, the fixture in the ceiling boasting three light bulbs of different colors. When he was a boy, he had done his homework in the parlor, stretched out on the floor. There had been no television in those days. In those days, the "William Tell Overture" had announced the arrival of the Lone Ranger. In those days, there was Omar the Mystic, and The Witch's Tale, and Renfrew of the Mounted, and, of course, on Sundays – the Shadow. He had grown up with the idea that Lamont Cranston was the most glorious name in the entire world. He now laughed whenever anyone mentioned it and yet, despite his sophisticated laughter, the name still touched a core of envy and awe somewhere deep within him. Lamont Cranston – the Shadow. Memories of a boy, the howl of a wolf and then the words, "Rennnnnnn-frew offfffff the Mounnnnnnn-ted," Dick Tracy every afternoon at – five was it? – five-fifteen? – milk on the kitchen table and chocolate-covered graham crackers, the memories of a boy. And now, the same living-room, called a "parlor" as it was in Puerto Rico, the same colored lights in the ceiling fixture, the same peeling paint, the same long tred through a railroad flat, a man entering a bedroom which could have been the twin of the one he'd slept in as a boy, and a man coming face to face with a boy of sixteen, and seeing in that face pain and trouble, trouble in the eyes and the mouth, and Hernandez the man suddenly wondering where Hernandez the boy had gone. And wondering what had been lost somewhere along the way.

"This is Frankie Hernandez," Mrs. Gomez said.

The boy regarded him without hostility. But there was determination in his eyes, a stubborn committment to reveal nothing. Hernandez had seen this look before. He had seen it in the squadroom and it had been worn by hardened criminals and by docile housewives; it was the same look, it never varied. It was a look which plainly stated, "You are the Law, and anything I tell you will be held against me."

"Hello, Alfredo," Hernandez said.

"Hello," the boy answered warily.

"Your mother's worried about you."

"She hass nothin' to worry abou'."

"Well, she seemed to think so. Came all the way over to the police station because she thought so. What about it, Alfredo?"

Alfredo sighed deeply. "I'm goin' to church, Mr Hernandez," he said. "I got nothin' to tell you."

"Your mother thinks you've got plenty to tell me."

"My mother doesn't know. She don' know this neighborhood."

"*I* know this neighborhood, Alfredo," Hernandez said flatly, and their eyes met, and in the boy's eyes was a recalculation now, a quick estimate of Hernandez's knowledge of the streets, an appraisal of the extent to which he was a neighborhood boy, and the extent to which he was a cop like all the rest. "Now what's all this about?" Hernandez asked.

Alfredo made his decision in a single moment. The decision changed nothing. Hernandez could not help him, Hernandez was the law, there was nothing he could tell him. "It ain't abou' nothin'," he said.

"Your mother said somebody's going to kill you, is that right?"

Alfredo did not answer.

"Answer me!" Hernandez said, and he seized the boy by the shoulders and forced the contact, forced eyes to meet eyes levelly and honestly. "Answer me!"

Alfredo remained mute, his eyes probing Hernandez's. And then he nodded.

"Who?" Hernandez asked.

"The ... the boys," Alfredo answered. His shoulders ached where Hernandez gripped him. His eyes remained locked with the detective's.

"Why?"

"No reason," Alfredo said.

"Is there a girl involved in this?"

"*Sí.*"

Hernandez released his grip tiredly. This was an old story, and he had heard it many times before. "What'd you do to the girl?" he asked.

"Nothin'."

"Come on."

"Nothin'."

The room went silent again. Hernandez stared at the boy. Patiently, he asked, "Then why do they want to kill you?"

"To show they big shots, thass all," Alfredo said. "They tink iss big to kill." He paused. He was talking more freely now, but he still wondered how far he could trust Hernandez. In a very low voice, he said, "She ain' even his girl. China ain' nobody's girl."

"You must have done something to the girl!" Hernandez said angrily.

"Nothin'! I swear! I swear on my mudder's eyes. Nothin'! I ony say hello to her. She a nice girl, smilin' an' everything, she smile at everybody. So I say hello. Iss somethin' wrong with dat? On the islan', you could say hello to girls, nobody bodder you. So now I am come here the city, an' now I cann say hello."

"How long have you been in this city?" Hernandez asked.

The boy shrugged and turned to his mother. "Mama?"

"He's a year now," she said. "We took the girl over first. His sister. Alfredo we left with his grandmother in San Juan. A year ago, we could afford to bring him here, too."

"Where's the girl now? Your daughter?"

"She belongs to the Girl Scouts. Today, they went on a picnic. Honeyside Beach, you know that?"

"Yes," Hernandez said. "You like this city, Alfredo?"

"Sure. I come from La Perla, thass where my gran'mudder lives. La Perla, thass a big *fanguito* in San Juan. A slom, you know? Shacks."

"I know La Perla."

"It means The Pearl, but thass jus' a joke, you know? It's not sush a pearl. Here iss better. Not so poor, you know? There, it iss all dirty an' mud, an' iss poor all the time. Here iss better." He paused. "But what can you do here?"

"You can do a lot here, Alfredo."

"Yeah? You go outside the neighborhood, they call you 'spic.' It's my fault I cann speak English so good? How I'm spose to learn? There's only one teacher in all my high school who speaks Spanish!"

"Others have learned English, Alfredo."

"Sure, I know. I'm tryin', ain' I? I do pretty good, don't I?"

"You do fine."

"Still..."

"Still what?"

"Am I ... am I spose to join a gang or somethin'?"

"Do you belong to a gang now, Alfredo?"

"No, I don' belong no gang. In Puerto Rico, we don' have this bullshit, these gangs like here. In Puerto Rico, you can say hello to girls, you can hang aroun' like whoever you want, you know? An' there's none of these dope. The kids here take dope. So I don' wann take dope, an' I don' wann belong to no gang. I ony wann to go my own way, nobody should bodder me."

"So how'd you get into this mess?" Hernandez asked.

"I say hello! I swear to God, all I say is hello! So Zip, he..." Alfredo cut himself short.

"Who?" Hernandez said quickly.

Alfredo was silent for several seconds. Then, as if finally committing himself, he said, "Okay. Zip. He sees me an' he says I bodderin' his girl. He says I don' go to church or they wash me."

"You ever been in trouble with this Zip before?"

"Once or twice. Like he try to shake me down at school, you know? We go the same school."

"What school is that?"

"A trade school. I'm learn a job."

"What kind of job?"

"Automotive. But thass not what I wann to be."

"What do you want to be?"

"I wann study radio. So when I wass in junior high school, I go the adviser, you know? I say, 'I wann study radio.' She tell me I should be an automotive. She says

iss better for a Spanish kid. She says iss better opportunity. But I still wann study radio."

"Why don't you tell this to someone at your school?"

"Oh, I don' know. Who's to listen? Sometimes I feel ... I
don' know ... like as if bein' here I'm jus' ... not a real human
bein', you know? Like I feel ... secondhand."

Hernandez nodded. "What happened with this Zip? When
he tried to shake you down?"

"Oh, I give him my lunch money," Alfredo said. "It wass
ony a quarter. I dinn want bad blood with him."

"And that was the extent of it? And you haven't had any
trouble with him since that time?"

"Never. Like he's ony new aroun' here, you know? Maybe he
lives here fi', six months. He come from somewhere downtown,
you know? So I don' bodder with him, I ony want to go my
own way, thass all. I don' like this ... I mean ... look, they
go aroun' stomping people ... they have these street bops ...
what I got to fight for? For what? I'm here this city now, so
here should be better, not *worse* than Puerto Rico. So why I
got to bodder with kids like Zip? He thinks to be big is to
kill." Alfredo paused and then stared solemnly at Hernandez.
"To be big is to *live*, no?" he asked.

"Yes, Alfredo."

"Sure. But he's leader of the Latin Purples. So I don'
belong no gang, no Royal Guardians, no Spanish Dukes,
nothin'. So who's to protec' me?"

"*I'm* to protect you, Alfredo."

"You? What can you do? You tink they afraid of cops? If I
don' show in the street, they call me turkey, they say I afraid
of them. So den everybody laugh at me. So den how can I
walk the street? If I be turkey, how can I walk the street?"

"It's not turkey to want to live, Alfredo. Every man wants
to live."

"I tell you the truth, I'm tired," Alfredo said. "I'm tired of
walkin' alone. You walk alone, they all pick on you. But I'm

spose to join a gang? I'm spose to go aroun' shootin' people? What for I want to shoot people?"

"Don't leave the apartment today, Alfredo," Hernandez said. "You'll be safe here. I'll see to that."

"And tomorrow?" Alfredo asked. "What about tomorrow?"

"We'll see. Maybe this'll all be cleared up by tomorrow."

"Will tomorrow be any better?" Alfredo asked. "Tomorrow I'm still here. I'm always here in this neighborhood." He began to weep suddenly and gently. "Always," he said. "Always here. Always."

There were four squad cars in the street outside when Hernandez got downstairs. They formed a loose cordon about the bar called La Gallina, and Hernandez immediately wondered if a Vice Squad raid was in progress. The street was filled with people who seemed to gather immediately at the sign of any excitement, who stood speculating in small knots outside the barrier formed by the squad cars on either end of the bar. Hernandez pushed his way through the crowd, saw that Parker was standing and talking to Lieutenant Byrnes and Steve Carella, who stood leaning against a fender of one of the squad cars. His first thought was *Who's minding the store?* and he realized instantly that this was no vice raid, that something big must have happened. Quickly, he walked to where the other detectives were standing.

"When do we start, Lieutenant?" Parker asked. There was a glow in Parker's eyes. He reminded Hernandez of a Marine who had been in his outfit. The guy's name had been Ray Walters, and he had joined the company on the day before the Iwo Jima landings. He hated the Japanese, and he couldn't wait for the landings to begin. He was the first man out of the landing barge, his eyes glowing, a tight grim smile on his mouth. The smile was still there when the Jap bullet took him between the eyes.

"We're getting cars on the next block," Byrnes said, "so we'll have radio contact with the men there. We'll start as soon as they're ready. This isn't going to be a picnic. He said we wouldn't take him alive."

"Are we sure it's him?" Parker asked.

"Who knows? We got a telephone tip. If it *is* him, we can't take any chances."

A woman came out of the tenement doorway to the left of La Gallina. She was carrying a baby in one arm and a bird cage in the other. A blue parakeet fluttered wildly about the cage. The woman came off the stoop, glancing over her shoulder to the windows above La Gallina. She seemed to sense that she was a star performer stepping into the spotlight and that an impatient audience was waiting for the one line she had to deliver, a line which would suddenly solve and resolve doubts and uncertainties which would have been mounting ever since the curtain rose. She stopped in the middle of the street, faced the crowd that milled restlessly beyond the squad cars and, in her loudest voice, shouted, "Ees Pepe! Ees Pepe Miranda up there!" and then she extended the bird cage, pointing with it to the first-floor windows while the bird fluttered and screamed against the brass bars.

"Come on, lady," a patrolman said, "before you stop a bullet."

The woman rushed into the crowd where the whisper had already gone up, a confirming whisper passed from mouth to mouth, accompanied by a knowledgeable shaking and nodding of heads, "Pepe Miranda, Pepe Miranda, Pepe Miranda."

"Is that what this is?" Hernandez asked Byrnes.

"It looks that way, Frankie," Byrnes said.

"Who called in the tip?"

"Don't know," Carella said. "He gave the info and then hung up."

"I'm going to see what the hell's happening with those other cars," Byrnes said. He walked around to the other side of the squad car, sat with his legs out on the street, and picked up the hand mike. "This is Lieutenant Byrnes," he said. "We're about ready to roll here. Are those other cars in position yet?"

"So we finally cornered your *landsman*," Parker said, grinning. "And we're gonna kill him. I'm personally gonna see to that."

"He's no *landsman* of mine," Hernandez said.

"Of course not," Parker answered. "That's just a way of speaking. All I meant was you're both Puerto Ricans."

"Sure."

"Hell, you know me better than that. I don't care if a guy's Puerto Rican or even Chinese."

"Sure."

Parker looked around suddenly. "Boy, look at these kids, will ya? They think Miranda's a god."

"He's only a god to the ones who don't know any better," Carella said, looking at the kids who had joined the crowd around the squad cars. The kids ranged in age from toddlers to adolescents. Some of them tried to climb onto the squad cars, but the patrolmen swiped at them with their night sticks. None of the kids seemed certain as to what sort of behavior was expected of them. Some laughed, and some stood solemnly staring at the first-floor windows of the building. Some seemed on the verge of tears. It was curious to watch their faces and to study their fidgeting. Each of them knew that this was an occurrence of unusual interest, and each of them was quite naturally excited by it. But they had seen many things, these children, and their reactions to all of these things had always been mixed. They had seen sudden blood, and every fiber in their bodies had urged them to scream at the sight of a man leaking his life onto the pavement, but fear had coalesced in their throats and erupted into the laughter of bravado. For these children, the emotions had become confused, with vague boundary lines separating one from the other. Fear was a twin to courage; tears and laughter were interchangeable.

"He's gonna be a *dead* god soon, that's for sure," Parker said. "He's gonna pay for every damn heartache he ever gave this city."

Carella, watching the children, said simply, "The city gave him a few too, Andy."

"Sure," Parker agreed. "It's the neighborhood. A kid grows up here, what the hell do you expect? Miranda was cutting up people before he knew how to walk."

"Maybe nobody ever took the trouble to teach him to walk," Hernandez said.

"Hey, you ain't getting sore at *me*, are you?" Parker asked, his eyes opening wide. "I thought he was no *landsman* of yours."

"He isn't. He's a punk. He's going to die. That doesn't make it all his fault."

"I can understand how you feel," Parker said. "There's a blood tie that..."

"There's no blood tie between me and..."

"I didn't mean a real blood tie, for God's sake. I know he's not your relative or anything. But, you know, you're both Spanish. That sort of makes you brothers, you know what I mean?"

"No. What the hell *do* you mean, Parker?"

"Aw, forget it. If you're gonna get sore, there's no sense talking. You're the touchiest guy I know, Frankie. I mean it. You oughta get over that. It don't help you none, believe me." He smiled at Hernandez and put his arm around his shoulder. "All I was saying, in a manner of speaking, is that I'm gonna kill your brother up there. I'm gonna put a dozen bullets in his goddamn skull and watch him bleed all over the sidewalk."

Hernandez shook the arm free. "You know something, Parker?"

"What?"

"He's more *your* brother than he is mine."

A half-dozen patrolmen had begun erecting barricades across the street. The people crowded the barricades. The kids began sitting on them, spilling over onto the side where the policemen and the squad cars waited for the word from the next street. Byrnes came out of the squad car and yelled, "All right, everybody *back! Step back!* Back of the barricade! Let's *go!*" He walked rapidly to Hernandez, pulling a handkerchief from his back pocket and wiping at his sweating face. "Frankie, do me a favor, will you?" he said. "Make with some Spanish. These people are gonna get shot up if they don't respect that barricade. Get them to move back, will you?"

"Sure," Hernandez said. He moved up to the wooden horses with their supporting crossbars, the stenciled POLICE DEPARTMENT letters shrieking against the white paint. *"Bueno!"* he shouted. *"Todos retroceder, Detrás de la barricada! Todos retroceder!"*

The crowd began moving back from the barricade. On the edge of the crowd, Zip grabbed Cooch's arm and said, "You hear that? You hear what that bull said? There's gonna be shooting!"

"With Miranda up there, there's gotta be shooting," Cooch said, his eyes wide.

"Who's Miranda?" Papá asked.

"Don't you know nothing, you dumb tiger?" Cooch said, shoving at him. "Miranda's the greatest thing ever happened to this neighborhood." He turned to Zip. "How you like this jerk? Don't know Miranda."

Zip shook his head, his eyes searching the first-floor windows for a sign of life. He could see nothing.

"When he lived around here," Cooch said to Papá, "this neighborhood really jumped, I kid you not."

"Even in my old neighborhood we knew about him," Zip said, his eyes never leaving the first-floor windows. "He was down there once, you know. I seen him. He was driving a big yellow Caddy."

"No crap?" Cooch said.

"Sure, I seen it. And he had this blonde with him. Man, you could see she was gassed completely out of her skull, just being with him. This was before things got so hot for him. Man, he was swinging then, swinging."

"A Caddy, huh?" Cooch said. "That's for me. Give me the wheel, man. I'll know just what to do with it."

"You should see the way this guy walks, Cooch," Zip said. He stepped away from the barricade and did a quick imitation. "This real cool glide, you know? Like he owns the world. That's the way to walk. Pepe walks with his head up. He ain't afraid of nothing or nobody!"

"Look at the way he got out of that Riverhead apartment!" Cooch said. "A dozen cops, and they couldn't touch him."

"Nobody can touch him," Zip said.

"Man, when he lived here, Zip, you shoulda been here, I mean it. A nice guy, you know? I mean, you think him being a big shot an' all, like he'd think us kids was dirt. But he was always nice to us, I swear. Used to hand out nickels, like that, you know? And stories? Man, the stories he used to tell us. You know, real straight-from-the-shoulder stuff. Not like the crap you get from your people."

"Man, I read you," Zip said. "If my old man gives me his pitch about the island one more time, I'm gonna lose control. Who gives a damn about customs on the island, huh? Who cares about the *hospitality* there, or the *sunshine* there, or the way the people close the doors when a stiff goes by, huh? This is *here*, man! This is where people are *living!*"

"You can bet Pepe knows how to live."

"Ohhh, brother, does he? This cat knows *the* story, dad! Hey, hey, look at that!"

"What?" Cooch said.

"Over there."

Two patrolmen were entering the tenement. They moved cautiously and with their revolvers drawn.

"It's about to start," Zip said, straining to see over the heads of the people in front of him. "We gotta get something to stand on, Cooch. We won't be able to see nothing this way."

"What about our other business?" Cooch asked.

Zip glanced cursorily over his shoulder, looking into the luncheonette where Jeff sat at the counter. "The sailor? Forget him. We scared him half to death."

"I mean Alfie," Cooch whispered.

For a moment, Zip seemed to have forgotten something that had kept him awake most of the night, something that had accompanied him as he'd got out of bed this morning, roaring in his mind as he dressed. For a moment, Zip seemed to make no association with the name "Alfie" and puzzlement showed plainly on his face. And then, as if being called away from something which was extremely pleasant and entertaining to take care of some simple task which was at best boring, he said, "Well, what about him?"

"We got a date, remember?"

"Of course I remember," Zip said angrily. "But how we gonna get to the church? The block's shut off. Besides, the kids with the pieces are on the other side of the street."

"Iss better this way, Zip," Sixto said. "We let heem . . ."

"Oh, shut up, will ya, Sixto?" Zip snapped. "Man, where'd we scrounge up this yo-yo?"

Papá burst out laughing. "You a yo-yo, Sixto," he said.

Cooch looked thoughtful for a moment. Then he said, "Zip, I can cut around the avenue and reach the kids that way. I can get those pieces for us."

Like a business magnate who cannot be bothered by a petty administrative detail, Zip answered, "Yeah, good. Go ahead, get them. Bring them back here." His eyes wandered up to the first-floor window again. "Man, I wonder how many pieces Miranda has in that pad with him."

"They say he took guns from all them cops in the..."

"Oh, man, this is gonna be the unholiest! Jee-sus, is he gonna give it to them bastards! Go ahead, Cooch. Go get the pieces. Come on Sixto!"

"Where we going?"

"Get something to stand on. There's always a million boxes in that empty lot on..."

The shots exploded from inside the building, a short volley with the echoing roll of distant thunder. The crowd went instantly silent. The silence hung over the street, and then was shattered instantly when a woman in the crowd screamed. An instant chorus went up after the scream, filling the street. A wisp of smoke drifted from the mouth of the building. The smoke hung on the air for an instant, silencing the crowd again, as if they had been a crowd in St. Peter's Square waiting for the smoke to rise from the Sistine Chapel, announcing the new pope, and now that they had seen the smoke, they still did not know who the pope was, and so they fell silent, and they waited.

From inside the building, a voice shouted, "Lieutenant! Lieutenant!"

9

The policemen on the rooftops and on the fire escapes, dangling from open windows perched behind parapets, seemed like a band of monkeys who had climbed into an intricate zoo gymnasium and now didn't know what to do with themselves. To say that Pepe Miranda was completely surrounded would certainly have been the understatement of the century. There were two tenements facing La Gallina, within the rather narrow confines of the cordon. These two tenements bristled with cops of every size, shape and rank – and each of these stalwart defenders of the peace was carrying a loaded and drawn revolver. An additional armory which seemed sizable and formidable enough to have stormed the gates of Stalingrad included such choice delicacies of destruction as rifles with affixed telescopic sights, submachine guns, regulation hand grenades, gas masks, tear-gas pellets, and even a flame thrower or two.

Nor did the siege confine itself to the two buildings facing La Gallina. The police had moved into the adjoining block as well, entering apartments which faced the back windows *on Sunday.*

of the apartment in which Miranda, like an animal driven into a hole, was trapped. Clean white wash fluttered on the back-yard lines. Policemen leaned out of open windows, pistols drawn, peering between the fluttering underpants and brassieres. There were policemen facing the front of the apartment and policemen covering the back of it, and policemen on the roof of the building itself, ready to descend upon Miranda from above.

The adjoining rooftops were covered with the citizenry of the city. Like a bunch of hicks who had come to see a circus daredevil dive eight hundred feet into a thimbleful of water, the people of the neighborhood were anxious to see whether or not Miranda could make the dive without splattering his brains out on the sawdust. To many of these people, Miranda was simply the rebel and the underdog. Consciously or not, they were rooting for him. They wanted him to stand up to this formidable army of men in blue, blast his way out of that goddamn apartment, tip his hat, throw a kiss to the ladies, and ride off into the sunset. Perhaps all of them knew how it would really end. Perhaps they all knew that a single man, no matter how mighty, could not withstand such forces arrayed against him. But many of them nurtured the secret hope that for once, just for once, the rebel would win, the revolutionary would defeat the incumbent dynasty, the anarchist would throw his bomb and escape.

For many others, there was an undeniable cultural tie between themselves and the man in the apartment. The tie was a curious one in that they all knew Miranda was a criminal. In all probability, none of them would have welcomed Miranda into their homes. He was a dangerous man, an unreliable man, a thief and a murderer. But he was Spanish. And, in much the same way that they took pride in the work of Pablo Picasso, they took a strangely curious pride in the fact that Miranda was causing so much excitement. In their minds, there was a very thin line between fame and infamy. Miranda, whatever he had done, was a celebrity. And he was a celebrity whom most of his audience knew on a first-name basis.

For the others who watched, there was only curiosity. A man was trapped in an apartment. The other men wanted to get him out of that apartment. This was a baseball game. There were no good guys or bad guys, only two teams which were trying to win.

At the moment, Miranda's team seemed to have scored the first run. The cry of "Lieutenant! Lieutenant!" which had come from the hallway of the tenement was followed almost immediately by the sight of the man who'd shouted the words. He was a police sergeant, and he had a patrolman's arm draped over his shoulder as he dragged him into the street. The patrolman had been shot. The blood on his blue shirt was plainly visible even to the people who crowded the edges of the rooftops. The sergeant carried the man out and put him on the ground beside the radio motor patrol car. The cop inside the car immediately picked up the hand microphone and requested an ambulance. The crowd watched all this with the eyes of prophets who are noting an interesting development, but who are aware that the final outcome will have little or nothing to do with this minor incident. Miranda had shot one of the cops. That was interesting. But the fireworks were yet to come. Patiently, they awaited the fireworks. It is a rare year that has two Independence Day celebrations.

Standing alongside the wounded patrolman, sweating profusely, Lieutenant Byrnes asked, "How bad is it, Sergeant?"

"His shoulder, sir," the sergeant said. He paused, catching his breath. He was a big beefy man with graying hair. His uniform was a little too tight for him, but he didn't want to buy a new one because he expected to retire next year. When a man pays for his own working clothes, he's apt to consider replacements carefully. "Sir, you shoulda heard Miranda," he said, wedging the words in between his gasps for breath. "We was just making sure all the tenants was out of the building, sir. He began cursing in Spanish and shooting through his door. He must have fired about six shots. Two of them clipped Cassidy."

Byrnes stared at the man lying in the street. "Well, we're getting an ambulance, Sergeant. Stay with him, will you? Do whatever you can to make him comfortable."

"Excuse me," a man on the other side of the barricade said. He was a tall, thin man with penetrating blue eyes. He wore a tan tropical suit and a blue straw Panama. "Did I understand the sergeant to say...?"

"Who the hell are you?" Byrnes asked.

"I'm a reporter. I work for the city's largest afternoon tabloid. I couldn't help overhearing..."

"I know your paper," Byrnes said flatly.

"Did I understand the sergeant to say..."

"I'm busy, mister," Byrnes replied, and he went around to the other side of the squad car and picked up the hand mike.

"Nice guy, your *landsman*," Parker said to Hernandez. "Couple of inches lower, and Cassidy'd be dead."

"I didn't do the shooting," Hernandez said. "Miranda did."

"So who's blaming you? Listen, every race has its crumbs, ain't that so?"

"Knock it off, Parker."

"Ain't nobody blaming *all* the Puerto Ricans for a foul ball like Miranda. Look at yourself, for God's sake. Didn't you come from this neighborhood? So look at you now. A detective third grade. It took guts to do what you did. Hell, think of all your own people you had to arrest."

"I do my job, Parker."

"No question about it. You're a good cop, Hernandez. And it sure don't hurt to talk Spanish in a precinct like this one, does it?" He began chuckling. "Listen, who cares if you're taking unfair advantage of the rest of us poor slobs? You keep on the way you're going, and some day you'll be commissioner. Then your father can hang another picture in his candy store."

"Why do you needle me, Parker?"

"Who? Me? I needle you?"

"Why?"

"I don't needle nobody," Parker said innocently. "I'm just like you, pal. I do my job."

"And what's your job?"

"My job is keeping the streets clean. I'm a street cleaner with a gun. That's a cop's job, ain't it?"

"That's not *all* of a cop's job."

"No? Maybe you think I should go around holding junkies' hands, huh? I used to be that way, Hernandez. I used to be the kind of cop who felt sorry for people. Used to break my heart to tag a car even."

"I'll bet it did."

"You don't have to believe me. Ask any of the old-timers at the station. But I learned my lesson, all right. I learned my lesson."

"How?" Hernandez asked.

"Never mind," Parker answered, and he turned away.

He had been turning away for a long time now, for fourteen years, to be exact. He had been turning away from his duty as a cop, and from his duty as a man, but he excused his negligence by telling himself that he had once been the kind of cop who'd felt sorry for people, and that he'd learned his lesson since. There was a slight inaccuracy to his rationale. Andy Parker was not the kind of man who had ever felt sorry for anybody in his life. It was simply not in his make-up to exude sympathy for his fellow humans. What he probably meant was that one time he felt a closer identification with the people of the precinct than he did now.

And, to give the devil his due, Parker *had* once approached this somewhat elusive task of law and order with a distinctly different viewpoint. When he was a patrolman – though it never broke his heart to tag a car – he was inclined to be lenient with petty offenders, letting them off with a whack of his billet and a warning. There was, he had concluded, enough real crime going on in this precinct without persecuting decent people for minor infractions. He learned in those days that the law was open to interpretation long before it reached the law courts. He learned that the lowest arbitrator in the city's judicial system was a man who wore no legal robes at all; he was the patrolman on the beat. And so he handed down a dozen decisions each day, and his decisions definitely leaned toward giving the petty offender a break. At the same time, he felt he was tough and uncompromising with the out-and-out thief. He considered himself a good cop.

One day, the good cop who was Andy Parker was walking his beat when the proprietor of a dry goods store called him over. The man was holding the wrist of a young kid who had allegedly stolen a bolt of silk from the sidewalk stand. Parker questioned the owner, and Parker questioned the kid, and then he donned his judicial robes and said, "Well, we don't want to cause this kid any trouble, do we? Now, can't we just forget about all this?" The proprietor of the store was loath to forget about all this because the kid had allegedly passed the bolt of silk to an accomplice who had made his escape with the merchandise. But Parker kept administering his sidewalk practice, and finally everyone seemed satisfied to let the entire matter drop.

That evening, after he had changed to his street clothes, Parker went for a beer in a neighborhood bar. He had the beer, and he had a shot, and then he had another beer and another shot, and he was feeling like a pretty nice guy by the time he left the bar, and that was the last time in his life he ever felt like a pretty nice guy.

He was ambushed on his way to the subway by three men who didn't allow him the opportunity to draw his revolver. He was ambushed and beaten within an inch of his life. He lay on the sidewalk in a pool of his own blood, and when he regained consciousness he wondered *why* he'd been beaten or *who* had done the beating, and he drew what seemed to be the only logical conclusion. He figured that he had been beaten by friends of the shopowner because he'd let the kid get away with the theft of the silk.

He never did find out who had administered the beating on that lonely autumn night.

Perhaps it had been friends of the shopowner. Actually, it could have been any one of a hundred people who disliked Parker even in those days of amiability. Actually, it didn't matter who'd beat him up.

He learned several things.

The first thing he learned was that it wasn't nice to receive a beating. In the movies, a beating is usually a battle. The person getting the lumps is a fighting devil who manages to pick off a dozen of his assailants before he is finally subdued. Then he gets up, shakes the dizziness out of his head, wipes a trickle of blood from his lip, dusts off his clothes, and narrows his eyes, leaving the audience to speculate on just what that narrowing of eyes meant. In real life, a beating is very rarely administered with fists. The men who worked over Parker on that night in autumn were all as big as he was, and they were armed with sawed-off broom handles, and they really beat the piss out of him. They kept beating him long after he was unconscious, they beat him within an inch of his life, and the cliché happened to fit the situation well because they damn near beat him to death, and he may have been a lot closer than an inch to leaving the land of the quick. He had not liked that experience at all. So the first thing he learned was that he would never again, ever, as long as he walked the earth, be on the receiving end of a beating. Ever. He learned this the way a young boy learns his catechism. I will never again take a beating. I will never again take a beating.

And the way to be certain you will never take a beating is to hit first and ask questions later. It's handy to own a policeman's badge at such times. It makes apologies to innocent people easier afterward.

The second thing that Parker learned was that he was being entirely too easy and naïve in his approach to police work. From that day on, Parker would give a summons to anyone who so much as spat on the sidewalk. In fact, and curiously, from that day on Parker brought in more drunks, vagrants and innocuous offenders than any other cop working in the precinct. In his own eyes, Parker had stopped being a nice guy. He was a mean, tough son of a bitch, and he knew it. And if you didn't happen to like him, that was just too bad. Parker had a life to lead, and he knew how to lead it.

I will never again take a beating, he told himself.

I will never again take a beating.

In the luncheonette on the corner, Jeff Talbot held the wet handkerchief to the cut on the side of his face, wiping away the blood. Some of the blood had spilled onto the collar of his jumper, and he was already looking ahead to the scrub job he would have to do on it to get out the stain. Luís, behind the counter, was more concerned with the sailor's condition than with the excitement in the street outside. He watched the sailor anxiously, almost like a father.

"You all right?" he asked.

"I'm all right," Jeff replied. "What's that kid supposed to be?"

"Zip?"

"Is that his name? Yeah. Him."

"I don't know."

"I mean, what the hell, who was giving him any trouble? I was minding my own business."

"His business is minding other people's business. He'll wind up no good. Like Miranda up there."

"What I'm trying to get at ... well, what's he looking for trouble for? Is he hotheaded or something?"

Luís shrugged. "No more than most."

"Spanish people are supposed to be hotheaded, ain't they?"

"Some are, some aren't," Luís said, shrugging again.

"We ain't got a single Spanish person in all Fletcher, you know that?" Jeff said, a touch of surprise in his voice. "I never even *seen* a Spanish person until today, how do you like that?"

"I never saw anybody from Fletcher until today," Luís answered.

"What I'm trying to figure out..." Jeff paused, studied the blood-smeared handkerchief, and then looked up at Luís. "Well, *you* seem all right."

"All right?"

"I mean ... you ain't like him." Jeff paused. "That Miranda's Spanish too, ain't he?"

"*Sí.*"

Jeff said nothing. He nodded, and then seemed to fall into silent thought.

"If you figure that way, sailor, you will be making a big mistake."

"What way?"

"You know what way. That's the easy way to figure."

"This is pretty personal with me, Louise," Jeff said. "I *got* to know. I ain't doing this just for the fun of it. It's ... it's important to me."

"Why is it so important to you?"

"Because, well..." He looked at the clock on the wall, and he wondered if China would keep her date with him. And then he wondered if he still wanted to see her. He frowned and said, "It's just important to me, that's all."

10

Everyone seemed ready for whatever might lie ahead.

The police in the streets and on the rooftops and in the back yard were ready. The people watching the show were ready. Zip and Sixto had obtained a large packing crate from the lot on the corner and had set it up just beyond the barricade; *they* were ready. And even Lieutenant Byrnes seemed ready now. He apparently had learned that his forces were deployed exactly the way he wanted them. He held a large, battery-powered megaphone, and he stepped out from behind the squad car, put the cumbersome apparatus to his mouth, blew into it several times to test the volume, and then said, *"Miranda? Pepe Miranda? Can you hear me?"*

His voice echoed on the silent street. The people waited for Miranda's reply, but none came.

"Can you hear me?" Byrnes said again, his voice booming out of the speaker. Again, there was silence. In the silence, the crowd seemed to catch its breath together, so that something like a sigh escaped their collective lips. *"All right, I know you can hear me, so listen to what I'm*

saying. We've got this street and the next street blocked. There are policemen with guns in every window and on every rooftop facing that apartment, front and rear. You're trapped, Miranda. You hear that?"

Zip and Sixto clambered up onto the crate and peered over the heads of the crowd. "This is *our* box, you dig me?" Zip said. "Only for the Latin Purples. I don't want nobody else climbing on it."

"How about it, Miranda?" Byrnes said. *"You coming out, or do we have to come in after you?"*

"Why don't he answer?" Zip said impatiently. He turned to the first-floor windows, cupped his hands to his mouth, and shouted, "Answer him, Pepe!"

"If there's shooting around here," Byrnes said into the megaphone, *"some of these people in the street might get hurt. Now how about it, are you coming out?"*

There was another long silence. Byrnes waited.

"Okay," he started, *"if you . . ."* and the voice came suddenly from one of the first-floor windows. There was no body attached to the voice, no one visible in any of the windows. The voice seemed to materialize from nowhere, a shouted voice which rang into the street, cutting off the lieutenant's words.

"Who did I shoot?"

"It's Pepe!" Zip shouted, and the cry spread through the crowd like lava rushing down a mountainside, "It's Pepe, Pepe, it's Pepe, it's Pepe, Pepe, Pepe."

"You shot one of our patrolmen," Byrnes said.

"Did I kill him?" Miranda shouted from the apartment, still invisible, his voice floating down into the street.

"No."

"You're lying to me. I killed him."

"You hit him in the shoulder. Are you coming out?"

"Did I kill him? Is he dead?"

"Let them come after you, Pepe!" Zip shouted.

"Miranda, we don't want to play games here. If you're coming out..."

A new sound erupted, drowning out the words that came from the megaphone, filling the air with its familiar wail.

"What's that?" Miranda shouted.

"It's an ambulance. What do you say, Miranda?"

"He shouldn't have tried nothing with me," Miranda said. "He could have got killed. I could have killed him."

"But you didn't. So what do you say? Yes or no? You coming out?"

"No!" Miranda shouted, suddenly and viciously. "You think you got some cheap punk up here? This is Pepe Miranda!" His voice rose. *"You hear me?* You want me, you come in here and get me!"

"That's telling them, Pepe!" Zip yelled, and he poked Sixto in the ribs, and suddenly the street was alive with cheers of encouragement.

"Yea, Pepe!"

"Bravo, Pepe!"

"Tell 'em, tell 'em!"

"Quiet!" Byrnes roared. *"Everybody quiet!"* Patrolmen moved quickly into the crowd, and the people in the street fell suddenly silent. But the rooftops still rang with cheers for the trapped killer in the apartment. Byrnes waited for the sound to die out. He put the megaphone to his mouth and said, *"All right, Miranda. No more talk. We're coming in."*

"Then stop talking and come get me, you yellow bastards!" Miranda shouted, and suddenly the shade on one of the windows snapped up, and there he was, Pepe Miranda the killer, a short, wiry man standing in his undershirt, his lips pulled back into a snarl, a three days' growth of beard on his face, a gun in each hand. He pulled back his head, and then snapped it forward with a short jerking motion, spitting into the street. And then he began firing blindly, both guns blazing as if he were trying to prove he was the marshal of a tough Western town.

Byrnes waved at the rooftops, and an ear-splitting volley shattered Sunday like a piece of crystal. He scooted for cover behind the squad car while the guns roared down from the rooftops. In the crowd, women were screaming and men were ducking behind each other for cover. Byrnes waved his hand again. The volley stopped, Miranda was no longer at the window.

He gathered Carella, Parker and Hernandez around him. "Okay," he said, "we're moving in. This time Miranda bit off too big a piece." He paused and looked at the faces of the men around him. "Has Captain Frick arrived yet, Steve?"

"Yes. I saw him a little while ago."

"Let's find him. I want this to be right."

Frederick Block was on his way home when he suddenly found himself in the middle of a traffic jam. Block hated traffic jams, and he especially hated them on weekends. He had gone to his office downtown to pick up a carton of eyelets which a factory in Riverhead needed instantly. He had made the delivery himself – "When you deal with Block Industries, you get service," he had told his client – and had then taken the shortest route he knew from Riverhead to the Calm's Point Bridge, and that route happened to take him through the heart of Isola and the 87th Precinct. And now he was in the middle of a traffic jam, on a Sunday, sweating inside his automobile when he should have been at the beach. Block was a fat man. Not one of those fat men who try to kid themselves by applying euphemistic terms like "stout" or "chubby" to their obesity. He was fat. F-A-T. And being fat, he sweated a great deal. And being a person who sweated – fat men, Block knew, never *perspired* – he did not appreciate being locked in a parked car in the middle of Isola on a day like today.

He bore the heat with tolerant malice for as long as he could. Then he got out of the car and tried to find out just what the hell was causing the tie-up. As far as he could see, there had been no accident. It always annoyed the hell out of Block when there was an accident. In the first place, careful drivers didn't get into accidents. And in the second and more important place, even if the wrecked car itself didn't block the road, traffic always slowed down to a snail's pace because every passing motorist wanted to study the extent of the damage.

Today, there had been no accident. And yet traffic was tied up on the avenue in both directions. Now why? Block wondered. With the instincts of an old bloodhound, he followed the crowd. They all seemed to be heading in the same direction, and he assumed the prime attraction was in that direction. Waddling along, mopping his brow with a big white handkerchief, cursing mildly under his breath, Block made his way up the avenue, and stopped at the luncheonette on the corner. A sailor was sitting at the counter. Block sidled up to him and said, "What's going on, mate?" He had never been in the navy, but he was a born salesman who adapted his speech to fit any and all occasions. "Why can't I get my car through here? What's going on?"

The sailor did not answer. The sailor kept dabbing at his face with a wadded handkerchief. Block didn't see the blood on the handkerchief, so he assumed the sailor was hot and wiping away sweat. He sympathized with the sailor and turned to the man behind the counter.

"Can you tell me what's going on?" he asked.

"The traffic's tied up," Luís said.

"You're telling *me* it's tied up?" Block said, and he began chuckling, his layers of fat jiggling. "Say, what kind of answer is that? It's tied up downtown and uptown and probably crosstown, too. What's going on? A parade?"

"There's a gunman in the apartment up there," the sailor said suddenly.

"A what?" Block wiped his brow. "A gunman, did you say?"

"Pepe Miranda," Luís put in, nodding.

"I never heard of him. What'd he do, rob a bank?" Block said, and he began chuckling, the fat jiggling all over him again. He didn't look at all like Santa Claus.

"You live in this city?" Luís asked.

"Sure, I live in this city. Not around here, though. I live in Calm's Point. What is this Miranda, a celebrity?"

"He's a killer," the sailor said quietly.

"Yeah?" Block opened his eyes wide in appreciation. "Yeah? A killer?"

"That's what he is," Jeff said.

"They going up there to get him?" Block said.

"That's what it looks like. You better go back to your car, mister. There might be shooting around here."

"No, no," Block said, very interested now. "I want to watch this. I want to see him die."

He shoved his way through the crowd, using his huge stomach like a battering ram.

"Louise," Jeff said, "what time is it?"

"I don't know. Eleven-thirty, something like that. Why?"

"I'm ... I'm supposed to meet a girl here. At noon."

"Sailor, why don't you take your own advice? Get out of here before you run into more trouble. Take a walk over to the park, eh? When the girl comes, I'll tell her you're waiting there for her. What's her name?"

"China. That's a funny name, ain't it?"

"Not for a Spanish girl. Only in Spanish, it's pronounced Chee-na." Luís shrugged. "A lot of the girls today, they give it the English sound. Or maybe people do it for them, and then they decide it's easier that way." He paused. "Go. Go to the park. I'll tell her where you are."

"I thought she was a whore when I first met her, Louise. That's a damn rotten way to start off, isn't it?"

"Well, I know many men who have married prostitutes," Luís said. "They make good wives."

"Oh, she ain't!" Jeff said, almost shouting the words in his haste. "I didn't mean to give you that impression. I mean, you can see that, once you know her. She's got this ... this real sweet face, you know?"

Luís smiled. "*Sí.*"

"Yeah, like a little girl, you know?" He grinned at Luís and then quickly said, "Not that she doesn't look womanly. I mean, she certainly has all the ... the ... things a ... woman has."

"I have never seen an ironing board among Puerto Rican women," Luís said.

"Huh?"

Luís curved his hand through the air, pantomiming a woman with uncommonly pronounced curves.

"Oh, yes," Jeff said. "Sure. But she doesn't look sloppy, you understand that, don't you? I mean, she's not one of these..." He used his hands to indicate a woman whose upper portions were mountainous.. Both men nodded in solemn agreement on the proper size of a bosom. "She talks nice, too," Jeff said. "I like a girl with a good voice and ... and eyes that look at you. When she talks, I mean. She looks at you. That's good. It makes you feel like ... like you're important."

"*Sí*, a man must feel that he is important."

"That's what I didn't like about Fletcher, Louise. I just felt like anybody else there. It's funny but, well, meeting her I feel like – I don't know – I feel like *me!* That's pretty stupid, ain't it? I mean, like who the hell else would I feel like? And I hardly even know her. I mean, she's just another girl, isn't she?"

"Sure," Luís agreed, "she's just another girl. You can find girls anywhere."

"Well, now she's not exactly *just* another girl," Jeff said hastily. "She's prettier than most, you know."

"Pretty girls are easy to find, sailor. The world is full of pretty girls. And for every man in the world, there is one girl who is pretty."

"Sure, sure. But she's, well, I guess you could call her beautiful. I guess you really could, Louise." He paused. "Do you ... do you think she'll come?"

"I don't know," Luís said. "Perhaps."

"I hope so. Gee, Louise, I hope so."

From Zip's vantage place on the packing crate, he saw her at once, working her way through the crowd. He waved to her instantly, and then shouted, "Elena! Hey, Elena, over here!" He poked Sixto and said, "Hey, Sixto, it's Elena."

Softly, Sixto said, "I thought China wass your girl."

"Variety, huh?" Zip said, grinning. "Hey, Elena!"

The girl waved back. She was sixteen years old, an attractive girl with dark hair and dark eyes, wearing a skirt and blouse. The girl with her, slightly shorter than she, was wearing black tapered slacks and a boy's white shirt. "Hello, Zip," Elena called, and then said to her friend, "Juana, it's Zip and the boys."

Flatly, Juana said, "He's a terrifying creep."

"He's not so bad," Elena said. "Come on."

They walked over to the crate. Zip offered his hand to Elena and pulled her up beside him. Papá studied the chivalrous gesture, and then repeated it, offering his hand to Juana who took it with the disdain of a countess accepting aid from a doorman.

"You ever see anything like this, Elena?" Zip asked excitedly. "He shot one of them."

"Who shot one of them?" Elena asked.

"Pepe Miranda!" Papá said.

"Who?"

"Pepe Miranda," Zip said. "He's got a whole arsenal in that apartment with him. The cops can't figure how to get him out. Man you shoulda seen him. He come right up to the window and spit at the bastards!"

"Who's this?" Juana asked, turning her attention to Zip.

Papá, as if repeating a lesson he had learned, a lesson he *had* indeed learned earlier from Cooch, said, "He the grays thin' ever happen this neighborhood."

"Yeah?" Juana said aloofly. "I never heard of him."

"So *that's* what this is all about," Elena said. "We were walking over on the next block and everybody was heading here like somebody hit the numbers for a million dollars."

"There ain't no numbers on Sunday," Juana said distantly. She was not a very pretty girl, but she had learned somewhere that her eyes were very attractive and had further learned how to use make-up on them. Her eyes were the focal point of her face, as green as jade and, combined with her jet-black hair, they created an instant impression of desirability which overshadowed the true facts of her plainness.

"You came through the next block?" Zip asked Elena.

"Sure. Why not?"

"No reason." He paused. "That's Royal Guardian territory."

"So what?"

"Nothing. Nothing."

"Royal Guardians or not," Elena said, "this is a free country."

"We walk where we want to," Juana added.

"That's because you're a chick. It ain't so easy when you're a guy," Zip said.

"Why not?" Juana asked.

"Because it ain't, that's all. You can't go messing in another club's territory."

"That's nuts. Haven't you got anything better to do than play war? That's kid stuff."

"There's nothing kid stuff about it," Zip said. "You just don't know."

"I know plenty," Juana said. "You haven't got anything better to do, that's all. That's why you've got these territories and these street bops and..."

"I got plenty to do," Zip said. "We always got plenty to do, ain't we, Sixto?"

"Sure, he's got plenty to do," Elena said. "He's got China to chase after."

"Hey, listen," Zip said, grinning. "How about a hug, Elena?"

"If you had things to do," Juana persisted, "you wouldn't get involved in this childish nonsense. What you are is an acting-out neurotic."

"A *what?*" Zip said.

"An acting-out neurotic," Juana said professorially.

"How come you're so smart, huh? Where'd you get your medical degree, huh?"

"I read an article in the newspapers," Juana said smugly.

"Dig the big reader!" Zip said, and he burst out laughing. Dismissing her, he turned to Elena, "Hey, come on, no hug for me?"

"Go hug China," Elena said coldly.

"Come on, come on," Zip said, still grinning. But his grin seemed to have no effect on Elena. Deliberately she turned to Sixto.

"Who's your cute friend?" she asked archly.

"Huh?" Zip said.

"What're you?" she asked Sixto. "The strong silent type?"

"Me?" Sixto asked, bewildered by her sudden attention.

"What's your name?" she asked, moving closer to him, smiling the way she had once seen Jane Russell smile in a movie.

"Sixto," he answered.

"The article said you're insecure," Juana said to Zip.

"Don't give me any bull you read in the newspapers," he said, turning on her angrily, miffed by Elena's behavior. "I don't believe nothing I read."

"You probably don't even know *how* to read," Juana said.

The thing that was happening on the packing crate was rather odd. Because despite Juana's protests that Zip was a terrifying creep, an acting-out neurotic, and insecure to boot, her conversational efforts had all been directed at him. And even though her approach took the form of an attack, it was clear that she was bidding for Zip's attention and no one else's. Elena, meanwhile, was doing exactly the same thing, even though she seemed to be addressing Sixto. A none-too-subtle tug of war was taking place on that crate. Whatever Zip's flaws, he was obviously recognized by the girls as the most desirable of the three boys. And, thanks to either his indifference or his stupidity, he hadn't the faintest idea of what was happening.

"So how come you're so quiet?" Elena said to Sixto. "Aren't you excited about your friend Pepe Miranda?"

"He's no' my frien'," Sixto said. "Pepe's no damn good!"

The girl caught the accent. She looked at Sixto for a moment and then said, "Hey, what are you? A tiger or something?"

"I no tiger."

"You sound like one. Can't you speak English?"

Papá had been thinking over Sixto's comment, and had finally fathomed the meaning of it. "What you minn, he's no good?" he asked now. "Hey, Zeep! Sixto, he say Pepe's no good."

Zip turned from Juana. "What? Did you say that?"

"I dinn say nothin'," Sixto said.

And now Elena, anxious to recapture Zip's attention, quickly leaped in. "That's what he said, Zip. That's what the Marine Tiger said, all right."

"I no tiger. I speak English good!"

"He speaks a well English," Zip said, chuckling.

"He said Pepe's no good," Elena repeated.

"Is that what you said?" Zip asked, and he shoved out at Sixto. "Is that what you said, huh?" and he shoved again. "Huh?" and again he shoved, pushing Sixto closer to the edge of the crate. "Is that what you said, Sixto?" and he pushed hard this time, sending Sixto over the edge of the crate, reeling backward into the gutter. Zip burst out laughing. Papá and Elena joined him. Juana seemed undecided for a moment, as if her natural instinct was to climb down and help Sixto to his feet. The indecision passed. She tittered nervously, and then burst into laughter with the rest of them. Zip put his arm around Elena.

"What's wrong with you, anyway?" he asked.

"Nothing."

"So how come the big freeze?"

"What's with you and China?"

"That?"

"That."

"Nothing." He shrugged.

"The word says you're after Alfie."

"Well, like he's got it coming, you know?"

"Why? Because of something with China?"

"What're you worried about China for, huh?"

"*Is* there going to be trouble?"

"With Alfie?"

"Yes," Elena said.

"Naw, no trouble," Zip answered. "Don't worry, huh?"

"Have you got a thing on with China?"

"Me?" Zip began laughing again. "Hey, you're jealous, ain't you? I'll be damned."

"She's old enough to be your mother," Elena said sullenly. "She must be nineteen, maybe even twenty."

"That don't make her old, only experienced. What's the matter, honey, huh?" he said sweetly. "You jealous, baby, huh?"

"No."

"You worried about poor little Alfie?"

"I don't care what you do to Alfie. Just answer me one question."

"Sure, what's that?"

"You got eyes for China or not?"

"Like, you know, doll, your interest gasses me, but don't start strong-arming me. I'll bust you right in the mouth, you know?"

Juana turned to him suddenly. "It takes a big man, don't it, to hit a girl?"

"Oh, get lost, zombie," he said to her. He wrapped his arms around Elena. "Come on, where's my hug?"

"Zip, cut it out," she said. "There's people watching."

"So let them, who cares?" He took one arm from Elena and pointed into the crowd. "Hey! Hey you! Fat boy!"

Frederick Block, who had shoved his way up to the barricade, looked up at Zip.

"You watching us, Fat Boy?"

Block turned away with a look of extreme disgust on his face. Zip burst out laughing.

"See, honey?" he said. "Nobody watching us." He pulled her closer to him. "Mmmm, you are the softest girl."

"I shouldn't let you," Elena said. "Not after this China thing."

"Somebody's got to protect little China, no?" His hands roamed her body. He touched her breast, and she pulled away from him quickly, embarrassed, but he drew her close again, and she stood unprotesting in the circle of his arms. Zip stroked her back gently.

"You going to hurt Alfie Gomez?" Juana asked.

"Drop dead," Zip told her.

"Big man," Juana said. "Everybody in this neighborhood's a big man. It's just you're insecure, that's all."

"Man, she sprouts that crap like as if she grows it in her

mouth," Zip said. "I got news for you, zombie. I *am* a big man, now how about that? The Latin Purples ain't afraid of nothing or nobody!"

"Whoever heard of the Latin Purples outside of you and your mother?" Juana asked. "If one of those Royal Guardians came down the street right now, you'd pass out cold."

"I ain't afraid of no Royal Guardians," Zip said angrily. "I ain't afraid of *nobody!*" He searched in his mind for a clincher to his argument, and then blurted, "Why, one of my boys is out right now, rounding up a couple of pieces!"

"If one of them goes off accidentally, you'll run a mile."

"You better tell your pal to shut up, Elena," Zip warned.

"Juana, stop picking on..."

"A gun is a psychological symbol," Juana said. "You only want one because you're afraid."

"I ain't afraid to rap you right in the mouth," Zip said.

"Big man," Juana repeated, but she shut up.

Zip looked out over the crowd. "They're coming back," he said. "The bulls are coming back."

11

The plan was a simple one, but Lieutenant Byrnes had discovered in his years of police work that most feasible and practical plans *were* simple.

The plan was one of deception, a plan which would utilize every man's innate susceptibility to the expected, and then knock him flat by suddenly producing the unexpected. The plan, of course, undertook to presume what Miranda would consider "expected". But it seemed a reasonable guess to suppose that Miranda expected the cops to get him out of that apartment, and that one certain way to accomplish this was to bust into the joint. If a rush were made across the street, a rush which carried all the earmarks of a frontal attack, Miranda would brace himself for an assault on his front door. Actually, the assault would come from elsewhere. Such was the unoriginal and simple nature of the deception. Broken down into simple terms, the police plan could have been stated thusly: *Hit him where he ain't.*

"Have you got it straight?" Byrnes asked his men.

"I want the fire escape," Parker said.

"We'll see about that."

"I want to be the one who gets him," Parker said. "I want to blow his head off."

"Sometimes, Parker, you turn my goddamn stomach," Byrnes said.

"What?"

"Nothing."

"Well, what do you want to say something like that for?"

"Skip it," Byrnes said. "Do you understand the plan?"

"I understand it," Parker said sullenly.

"Frankie?"

"I've got it."

"Steve?"

"Run through it once more, would you, Pete?"

"Okay, this is it in a nutshell. I'm going to tell Miranda we're coming in after him. A pile of us'll rush the stoop when the shooting starts. Miranda – I hope – will think we're going to force the apartment door from the hallway. But one of us will break away from the rest and flatten himself against the side of the building."

"Me," Parker said.

"Whoever it is, he'll pull down the ladder of the fire escape and climb up to the first floor. He may be able to get Miranda from the window. Otherwise, he'll have to enter the apartment and have it out there. It's tricky, but I'd rather risk one man than a dozen."

"Let's get started," Parker said.

"In a minute. I need a volunteer for that fire escape job."

"You've already got your volunteer, Lieutenant," Parker said.

"You've got *two*," Hernandez said.

"Keep out of this, Frankie. This is my baby."

"Why should it be?"

"Because I want it."

"I'll decide who . . ." Byrnes started.

"Lieutenant, you'd be crazy to send up a guy who's..." Parker cut himself short.

"Who's *what?*" Hernandez asked.

"Okay! Who's got a personal stake in this, okay?"

"Personal? What the hell are you talking about?"

"You grew up with Miranda!"

"What difference does that make? We want him out of that apartment, don't we?"

"We want him *dead,*" Parker said. "He's a punk. He should have been killed a long time ago. He's the biggest stink in these streets."

"What the hell do you know about the stink here, Parker? Did you..."

"I seen plenty of it. I been in this precinct for..."

"Did you grow up with the stink in your nostrils, day and night? Did you live with it every day of your life?"

"You're telling me about this precinct? I know it like my own mother. There's nothing you can tell me about..."

"No, nothing! To you, this precinct is one big violation, one big crime being committed every hour on the hour. And you're scared of the place! You're scared out of your wits!"

"Scared? Who the hell..."

"Well to me it's *people!* And they deserve a goddamn break! They want to get that son of a bitch as much as you do!"

"They want him to hold off the whole damn city!" Parker shouted. "You know that! You know it's true!"

"They only want a Puerto Rican to win for a change. Okay, if I go up there, a Puerto Rican wins."

"If I go up..."

"If you go up, you purge yourself. You think killing him is gonna help you, Parker? You think that's the answer?"

"I don't know what the hell you're talking about."

"If you go up there, you accomplish nothing. Not for yourself, and not for the city. You'll be making Miranda a hero. I'm telling you that right now. You kill him, and this neighborhood has a martyr. The kids'll be playing *Pepe Miranda and the Cops* for the next six weeks."

"The hell with the kids. You think I'm interested in ... ?"

"Who's gonna show them, Parker? You want a hundred more Mirandas ten years from now?"

"*You* gonna show them?" Parker asked sarcastically.

"If I kill him," Hernandez said flatly, "the neighborhood gets nothing but a dead punk."

"You've got him, Frankie," Byrnes said.

"Thank you."

"Get to the car, Parker. Radio the men on the next block to open up. I want to draw his fire away from these windows."

"You're sending Hernandez up there?"

"Yes. Any complaints?"

"Damn right I've got a—"

"Take it to the mayor!" Byrnes snapped, and he turned his back and walked toward the patrolman who was holding the megaphone. Parker stared after him, spat viciously into the gutter, and then walked around to the other side of the squad car.

A reporter behind the barricade caught at Hernandez's sleeve. "Hey, are you in charge here?" he asked.

"No."

"Well, who is? Can't we get some men in there for pictures?"

"The police department'll send out pictures," Hernandez said. He pushed past the reporter and walked to the luncheonette. "Look at these kids," he said to Luís. "Sucking violence from the same tits Miranda used." He shook his head. "He's waiting up there to die, Luís, you know that? He's waiting up there for us to kill him."

Luís nodded.

"And you know something? I think he *wants* to die. I think he *wants* to end it, once and for all."

*   *   *

The two girls who came around the avenue and stopped at the mouth of the street were apparently more interested in beginning something than in ending it. They were both tall brunettes. One was wearing a tight, bright-red silk dress. The other wore the identical dress in yellow. The dresses were designed to exhibit and reveal; they were incapable of keeping a secret. Every nuance of flesh beneath the skintight silk, every subtle hint of muscle or bone, every flowing curve, every dimple, every pucker, insistently shrieked its existence to the most casual observer. The girls were not the bashful type. They moved with a fluidity of breast, hip, thigh and leg that aided the dresses in their task of nonconcealment. They were, in fact, so much the Hollywood concept of what a whore should look like that at first glance they seemed to be imitations. If there was one quality which every prostitute in the 87th Precinct shared, it was the ability to look like anything *but* a street walker. In most instances, the precinct whore was the best-dressed girl on the streets. Her careful grooming, more than any other attribute, was usually the one clue to her occupation.

These two were either new at the trade, or else they'd canceled their subscriptions to *Vogue* magazine. In any case, they walked directly to the barricade and stopped there. The girl in the red dress touched the arm of the nearest patrolman who turned, ready to start yelling, and then looked as if a movie queen had wandered into his bedroom by mistake.

"Excuse me, officer," she said in a tiny little voice, "but can't we get through here? We work right across the street."

"Where?" the patrolman asked.

"At La Gallina."

"What the hell do you do *there*?"

The girl in the red dress seemed at a loss for words. She turned to her companion. The other girl smiled at the patrolman sweetly and said, "We're in ... ah ... public relations."

"Well, I'm sorry, girls," the patrolman said. "My orders are to let nobody through this barricade unless he's a cop or a fireman. Now you two girls ain't cops or firemen, are you?" He grinned politely, thinking how clever he was being, and making a note to repeat his comment to the boys in the locker room when he checked in later.

"No, indeed," the one in the red dress said.

They moved away from the barricade.

"What now, Marge?" the one in the yellow dress asked.

Marge shrugged. "Let's hang around. It looks like a lively crowd. There may be something in it for us, Marie."

Marie looked skeptical. Together, walking with a hip-swiveling, crazy-socketing, ball-bearing, thigh-thrusting, leg-strutting motion that turned every head on the block, they began appraising the potential customers watching the siege. Marie raised an eyebrow at Marge, and Marge glanced in the direction she indicated.

They were both looking at Frederick Block, the fat man.

12

There are times when it must be nice to have a Cinemascope camera and stereophonic sound. There are times when it must be great to have a wide screen stretching across the front of the world, with things happening on every corner of that screen, with the eye gathering in all these things like a net sweeping the ocean floor. It isn't enough to say this and this were happening here, that and that were happening there. A city street is not a tiny canvas; a city street is not a page in a book. It is a tumultuous thing teeming with life, and you can't hope to capture life in a sentence or a brush stroke. The things that happened on that street, on that particular day in July, happened almost simultaneously, separate and distinct from each other, but nonetheless almost at the same time, so that there was a feeling of continuous motion, of one event overlapping and flowing into the next. The wide screen stretched the length of a city block. The life on that street stretched to the very edges of time.

Cooch stood on the steps of the building next door to the church.

China came down a flight of stairs and into bright sunshine.

A man selling ices entered the street at the opposite end.

Marge and Marie, the two prostitutes, approached Frederick Block.

Jeff Talbot looked at the wall clock and left the luncheonette.

Two boys wearing bright-gold jackets turned into the block.

The cops of the 87th rushed the doorway to the left of La Gallina.

These are the things that happened, minute overlapping minute, time lost and time replaced by the tireless eye of space. These are the things that happened...

Cooch stood on the steps of the building next door to the church. He had been standing there for ten minutes now, watching the people pour down the church steps and into the bright confused sunshine of the street. There were not many people left inside the church now. He looked at his wrist watch, and then studied the few stragglers again. He was certain that Alfredo Gomez had not left the apartment to attend mass this morning. But he would wait a few moments more, just to make sure.

Against his belly he could feel the hard, cold metal of the pistols he had retrieved from Chico and Estaban. The weapons made him feel very strong and very powerful. Too, he considered this independent reconnaissance an act of foresight worthy of a general. He would wait until everyone had come out of the church, and then he would go back to Zip with the guns *and* with a report on Alfie's whereabouts. This was acting above and beyond the call of duty. Zip would be pleased. And whereas it would not be as dramatic to catch Alfie in his house instead of on the church steps, Cooch didn't much care. The important thing was to wash the little bastard. That was the important thing.

Cooch had been thinking about it all week long, ever since Zip first got the idea. There were times when Cooch couldn't sit still, just thinking about it. There were two stimulating and contradictory feelings which rushed through Cooch's mind and body whenever he considered what they were about to do. The first of these was the very concept of killing. This excited him. He had fantasized the squeezing of a trigger many times, had imagined Alfie tumbling down the church steps, had wondered what it would feel like to know that he had killed another human being. He had convinced himself that Alfie deserved killing. He had, after all, messed with China.

This was the second idea, and this was as exciting as the first. A hundred or more times in the past week, Cooch had imagined Alfie messing with China. He wondered just what Alfie had done to her, and his imagination created new images each time. Alfie gently stroking China's full breast. Alfie unbuttoning China's blouse. Alfie thrusting both hands beneath China's skirt. Alfie...

The images continued to stimulate him. And they were images clouded with guilt. Lying alone in his bed at night, he would think of Alfie and China, and then he would roll over into his pillow and think *The son of a bitch has to die for that.*

Of that he was certain.

Alfredo Gomez had to die.

Standing on the steps of the tenement, he watched the last few stragglers leaving the church, and he thought again of Alfie and China, and he bit his lip and then thought of shooting the little bastard.

China came down a flight of stairs and into the bright sunshine.

The tenement hallway had been dark, and she blinked now against the sudden brilliance, knowing she still had at least five minutes before she was to meet the sailor, not wanting to get there too early or seem too anxious, and yet almost unable to control the forward motion of her feet as they took her onto the stoop. Jeff was his name. Jeff, Jeff, Jeff, her mind echoed, and her heart beat with the idea of the rendezvous, and she found herself gripping the shopping bag in her hand more tightly. She had wrapped chicken in wax paper, had put up some eggs to boil before going to church, had later packed the hard-boiled eggs, and salt, and fruit, and a thermos of iced coffee, all of which were in the shopping bag now. She wondered if he liked chick—

"Hello, China."

She blinked and then shielded her eyes from the overhead sun.

"Oh, hello, Cooch," she answered, and she smiled and began to walk around him, but he stepped into her path.

"I was just thinking about you," Cooch said.

"Oh?" China glanced at her watch. "Cooch, I haven't got time to talk to you right now. I have to..."

"About what we're going to do for you today."

"What? I don't under—"

"Alfie?" Cooch said, smiling.

"Alfie?" She paused, puzzled. "Alfredo, do you mean? Alfredo Gomez?"

'Uh-huh," Cooch said, nodding.

"What about him?" She looked at her watch. She would have to hurry. With all that police trouble up the street, she would have to cut around the avenue and that didn't leave much time to...

"We're gonna get him," Cooch said. "For what he done to you."

"What?" she asked.

"Alfie," he repeated.

"Yes, but what ... what did you say?" She studied his face. She was certain she had heard him correctly, and yet his words hadn't seemed to make any sense.

"For what he done to you," Cooch said.

"What do you mean?"

"You know."

"No. I don't know."

He had taken a step closer to her, and she had backed away from him slightly. Blocking her path to the steps, he moved closer now, so that she was forced to take another step backward, almost into the darkened hallway of the building.

"You know what he done, China," Cooch said.

She looked at his face. His face looked very strange. He was a very young boy with a ridiculously silly mustache over his upper lip, and she had always thought ... but now he ... he ... looked different somehow.

"I have a gun," he said suddenly.

"A—"

"A gun, China."

"What ... what..." She was forced to back away from him again, into the hallway this time. He stood silhouetted in the doorway of the building, the bright sunshine behind him. His hand moved. For a moment, she didn't know what he was doing. And then she saw the dull glint of metal.

"It's a Luger," Cooch said.

"Wh–what are you going to do with that, Cooch?"

"Kill Alfie," he answered.

"Kill...? Why? What for?"

"For what he done to you?"

"He didn't do anything to me!" China said.

"You know what he done, China." He held the gun up close to her face. "You know what he done."

She was truly frightened now. She did not want to retreat further into the hallway, but he kept moving closer and closer to her, and there was no place to go but back. For a crazy moment, she wanted to turn and run up the steps to her apartment. And then it was too late. He had stepped between her and the steps and was moving toward her again so that, in backing away from him, she stumbled toward the garbage cans stacked under the steps on the ground floor.

"Cooch, I ... I have to go," she said. "I don't know what you're talking about. Alfie didn't do anything to me. If you're angry at him because you think..."

"*This* is what he done, China," Cooch said, and his hand reached out for her.

She felt his fingers tighten on her breast, and she screamed, pulling away from him. His fingers clung. She thought her blouse would tear. Blindly, she brought up the shopping bag, swinging it at him, screaming, and then shoving her way past him into the bright sunlight again, rushing down the steps, still screaming, into the crowd.

A man selling ices entered the street at the opposite end.

"*Pidaguas!*" he called. "*Pidaguas!* Come buy some *pidaguas*."

Zip, standing on the crate, turned to watch the man who pushed through the crowd with his cart. "Hey, you want some ices?" he asked Elena.

"You got any loot?"

"Sure," Zip answered. "What flavor you want?"

"Lemon," Elena said.

"I'll have a lemon, too," Juana said.

"Oh, now she knows me," Zip said, leaping down from the crate. "Now it's buying time, she knows me. Okay. I'm the last of the red-hot spenders. Everybody gets ices!"

From the crate, Papá said, "Me, too, Zeep?"

"You, too, Papá! Everybody! Everybody gets *pidaguas* today! Hey, Mac, slow down! Don't you want no business?"

He went over to the cart and placed his order. He seemed happy as hell. He paid no attention at all to the detectives who stood not six feet from him.

"Where are your men, Andy?" Byrnes asked.

"Coming, sir."

Byrnes turned to Hernandez who stood staring up at the first floor of the tenement. "You scared, Frankie?"

"A little," Hernandez answered.

"I don't blame you." He paused. "This is the damnedest thing ever, isn't it? The last one I remember like this was back in 1931 when this guy Nelson O'Brien was holed up in an apartment on the North Side. I was a patrolman at the time. He held off a hundred and fifty cops for two hours that day. We were chopping holes in the roof and dropping tear gas down on him, but the bastard wouldn't give up. We wounded him three times, but he was still standing when we went into the apartment to collar him. Standing and cursing – but out of amo. He'd hidden both his guns in his socks, hoping to use them later for an escape. A real prize, he was."

Byrnes paused and stared at Hernandez. "I didn't feel so hot that day, Frankie."

"Why not?"

"They guy in the apartment was Nelson O'Brien." He paused again. "I'm Irish."

"Yes, sir," Hernandez said.

"But I'll tell you something, Frankie. The guys like Nelson O'Brien don't stop me from marching in the St. Paddy's day parade every year. You understand me?"

"I understand you."

"Good." Byrnes hesitated. "Take care of yourself on that goddamn fire escape," he said. "I wouldn't want to lose a good cop."

"Yes, sir," Hernandez said.

Byrnes extended his hand. "Good luck, Frankie."

"Thank you." Byrnes turned to walk back to the squad car. "Pete?" Hernandez called. Byrnes faced him. "Thank you," Hernandez said again.

Marge and Marie, the two prostitutes, approached Frederick Block. Block was pulling his handkerchief out of his back pocket, preparatory to mopping his face with it, when his elbow struck something very soft. He turned casually. The something very soft was covered with bright-red silk.

"Hello," Marge said.

"Well, hello," Block answered. "Quite a show, isn't it?"

"If you like this kind of jazz," Marie said.

"Well, it's pretty exciting," Block said. He studied the low-cut front of Marie's dress. Damn, if this girl didn't have the...

"There are plenty things more exciting than watching a cheap gunman get shot," Marie said.

"Like what?" Block asked, beginning to get the impression that this girl wasn't even wearing a brassiere.

"Can't you think of anything?" Marie said.

"Well ... I can think of a few," Block said.

"Whatever you can think of," Marie said, "we can manage."

Block studied the girls a moment longer. He mopped his face. Then, with a practiced eye, and a whispered voice, he asked, "How much?"

"For one of us or both?" Marie asked.

"Both? Well, I hadn't..."

"Think about it."

"I am."

"Think fast," Marge said.

"We like to work together," Marie said.

"The Bobbsey Twins down on the Farm," Marge said.

"We know things they don't even know in Paris yet," Marie said.

"We know things ain't even been invented yet," Marge said.

"How much?" Block asked again.

"Fifty for the afternoon, including the stretcher bearers."

"The what?"

"The stretcher bearers. To carry you out when it's over."

Block chuckled. "How much without them?"

"Twenty-five for me alone. My name's Marie. It's a bargain, believe me."

"I'll think about it," Block said.

"Come on, come on," Marie prompted.

"Can't you just wait a minute?"

"Love don't wait a minute, mister," Marie said.

"Not in July it don't," Marge added.

"Twenty-five's too high," Block said.

"Make it twenty, sport. A double sawbuck, what do you say?"

"You're on."

"Or vice versa," Marie said dryly. She turned to her friend. "Well, I'm set. Now what are *you* gonna do with all that love busting inside you, huh, Marge?"

Jeff Talbot looked at the wall clock and left the luncheonette.

It was fifteen minutes past twelve.

She wasn't coming. He'd been a jerk to think she'd keep the date. He went out into the street, thankful that he had worn his whites today. God what a hot day, why hadn't she kept the date, why in hell hadn't she kept the date? He wanted to hit somebody. He just for the hell of it felt like hitting somebody. You meet a girl like that maybe once in— Oh, the hell with it. Angrily, he stamped back into the luncheonette.

"I'm shoving off, Louise," he said.

"What?" Luís answered.

"She didn't show. I'm leaving."

"Good," Luís said, nodding. "You will be better off out of this neighborhood. There are other girls, sailor."

"Yeah, that's for sure," Jeff said.

He walked out of the luncheonette again. It was a damn shame, he thought, because ... well ... he'd almost found it. He'd almost, in the space of what was it, ten, fifteen minutes?

In that short a time, he'd almost found it, but of course he should have known. Nothing good comes easy. And yet, it had seemed so right, it had just seemed ... seemed right, where ... where eyes meet and ... and without touching ... without saying very much...

The hell with it!

He strode out of the luncheonette, and the first people he saw were Frederick Block and the two prostitutes.

Marge winked at him.

Jeff squared his hat and walked directly to the trio.

"Well, well, well," he said.

"Feel like a party, sailor?" Marge asked.

He hesitated for just a moment, his eyes roaming the street. Then he said, "Yes, goddamnit, I feel *just* like a party!" and he grabbed Marge's elbow, and the four of them turned the corner and went off up the avenue.

Two boys wearing bright-gold jackets turned into the block.

They stood with their hands on their hips for a moment. Both wore sunglasses, both wore their dark hair in high crowns. The bigger of the two, and the older – a boy of about twenty who stood a little over six feet tall – wore a silver identification bracelet on his right wrist. His name was Tommy. The other boy, nineteen and short by modern standards, was called Li'l Killer. His real name was Phil. He had never killed anyone in his life, but the name made him sound like a guy who'd cut out your liver for the price of an ice-cream soda. The tall one, Tommy, nodded at Phil and they walked directly toward the crate where Papá and the two girls stood craning their necks.

"Hey, kid," Tommy said.

Papá turned. "You talk to me?"

"Off the box," Tommy said flatly.

"Huh?" Papá said. "Wha'?"

"You heard him," Phil said. "Off the box. We want a view."

Papá looked down to where Sixto stood near the side of the crate.

"Sixto, go call..." he started, and Phil shoved out at Sixto before he could move.

"Stay put, sonny," he said.

"Don't hurt him, Li'l Killer," Tommy said. He chuckled. "Just cripple him."

"Listen, why do you want trouble for?" Elena said, looking past them to where Zip stood at the ices cart near the corner.

"Who wants trouble?" Tommy asked gently. "Li'l Killer and me, we asked your friend very politely to get the hell off that box, that's all. That ain't no trouble."

"That ain't no trouble at all," Phil said.

In that instant, Lieutenant Byrnes waved his arm at the rooftops, and the police opened fire. The firing was a precise, methodical operation designed to keep Miranda away from the front windows. At the same time, the distant echo of guns could be heard in the back yard, and over that, like a triangle player in a hundred-piece orchestra, the sound of shattering glass. Miranda appeared at the front windows for just an instant, looked into the street, saw what he was supposed to see, and ducked back into the apartment.

The cops of the 87th rushed the doorway to the left of La Gallina.

Miranda saw them the second before he ducked his head. Lieutenant Byrnes led the charge, shooting up at the windows as he ran. Behind him were Steve Carella and Andy Parker and half a dozen patrolmen, all with guns in their hands. Frankie Hernandez brought up the rear. One by one, the cops entered the tenement. Hernandez seemed to be following them and then, suddenly, at the last moment, he swerved to the right of the doorway and flattened himself against the front of the building.

At the same time, Captain Frick – who commanded the uniformed cops of the 87th – brought the megaphone to his mouth and shouted, "*We're coming in, Miranda! We're going to knock that front door right off its hinges.*"

There was no answer from within the apartment.

"*We're coming in, Miranda! We're coming up those steps right now!*" Frick shouted, and he hoped Miranda would buy it.

In the hallway, Byrnes, Carella, and Parker crouched on the steps. They could hear the gunfire outside, could hear shouts from the cops, screams from the crowd, the sound of glass breaking and wood splintering, the high whistle of slugs that caromed and ricocheted.

Outside, Frankie Hernandez stealthily moved past the glass front of La Gallina, working his way toward the fire escape.

The crowd was suddenly hushed.

The only sound on the street now was the explosion of the revolvers on the rooftops and in the windows facing Miranda's apartment.

She came around the corner hurriedly.

There were tears on her face, and her blouse had pulled free from her skirt, and she thought she could still feel the imprint of Cooch's fingers where he had touched her. It was twenty minutes past twelve, and she hoped against hope that Jeff would still be there, hoped he had at least the faith to realize ... to realize *what?* Tears streaking her face, she rushed into the luncheonette.

He was not there.

She looked at the empty stools, and then she turned to Luís and she said, "Luís, there was a sailor ..." and Luís nodded instantly.

"He left."

"I ... I couldn't get away and then ... the crowds in the street ..."

"He left," Luís said again.

She turned from him quickly and went into the street again. She could hear the pistol shots, thunder on a sunny day. "China, hey, China!" She wished it would really rain, she wished the skies would open and – "China, hey, don't you hear me?" – rain would come down to wash the streets, wash all the ...

"Hey! *China!*"

She looked up suddenly. "What? Oh – oh, hello."

Zip was standing by the ices cart, grinning.

"Hey, how are you, China?"

"Fine," she said. "I'm fine, thank you."

"You want some ices?"

"No. No, thank you, Zip."

He studied her. "What's the matter?"

"Nothing."

"You look like you was crying. Was somebody bothering you?"

She shook her head. "No, no."

"If anybody bothers you, you just let me know," he said. "I'll take care of them the way I'm gonna take care of Alfie."

"You leave Alfie alone!" she said sharply and suddenly, her eyes flashing.

"Huh?"

"Why do you want to hurt him? You have no right to hurt him!"

"Hell, I ain't afraid of *him!*" Zip said.

"Nobody said you were."

"It's just, he's got this coming, that's all."

"You know he didn't do anything, Zip. You *know* that."

"He done plenty! I'm gonna bust him wide open. I'm gonna ..."

She began crying suddenly and fitfully. "Why do you *talk*

that way?" she shouted. "Why do you have to sound so tough? Aren't you ever yourself? Can't you be *yourself?*"

Surprised by her sudden passion, he stared at her, speechless.

"What are you trying to show?" she asked, the tears running down her face. "What are you trying to do? Make it worse here than it really is? What's wrong with you? What the hell is *wrong* with you?"

He stared at her, confused. He reached out to touch her, not knowing that the tears were something which had been building inside her from the moment Cooch attacked her, building on the wild run from the tenement to the luncheonette, building against the desperate hope that the sailor would still be there, kept in check by sheer will power, and now overflowing; he did not know these things, he only knew that she was crying. And in the face of such female vulnerability, in the face of anguish such as he had never known or seen, Zip pulled back his hand, unable to touch her in that moment, unable to establish a contact which seemed in that moment too intimate, too revealing.

"Hey ... hey, listen," he said, "don't cry. What do you want to cry for?"

"Promise me you won't do anything to Alfie," she said. "Promise me."

"Listen ... hey, you don't have to cry."

"Promise me."

"China ... everybody knows what I said I was gonna do. Like I told them—" He hesitated. "I told them you was my girl."

"You shouldn't have said that."

"I know. I mean, even *I* know you ain't my girl. Listen, can't you stop crying? You want my handkerchief?"

"No," China said, sobbing. "I'm not crying."

"Here, take it," he said, handing her the handkerchief. "I hardly used it yet."

She took the handkerchief and blew her nose.

"You want some ices?" Zip asked lamely.

"No. Zip, you won't hurt him, will you? He did nothing to me, believe me. He's a nice boy."

Zip did not answer.

"You'll be doing something very wrong if you hurt him."

"You ain't sore at me, are you?" His voice dropped. "Like because I said you was my girl?"

"No. I'm not sore."

"I won't say it no more," he said gently. He shrugged. "I don't even know why I said it." He thought for a moment. "Except maybe because you're so nice, you know?"

"Thank you," she answered, and she smiled weakly. She handed him the handkerchief. "I got it all wet."

"Oh, that's okay, that's okay." He shrugged. "You feel a little better now?"

"A little."

"You really shouldn't cry, China. It's a sin to cry unless like something serious happens, you know? Like unless you lost somebody or something."

"I *did* lose somebody, Zip." Her eyes clouded for an instant, and then she shook her head. "You promised? About Alfredo?"

"Well, I didn't exactly..."

"I wouldn't want you to get into trouble," she said.

He stared at her as if she had uttered the words in Russian. His brow furrowed. He kept staring at her. The concept seemed new to him. Nor could he understand her concern. It wasn't as if she was struck on him or anything, he knew lots of girls who were, but China wasn't. So what was it? Why should she give a damn about him one way or the other? And yet, he knew she wasn't lying. Standing with her, he knew that she was as much concerned for his safety as she was for Alfie's.

"I got to think about it," he said.

"Yes, think about it. Please." She touched his hand briefly, and started off toward the corner.

He watched her go, a frown on his face.

"*Pidaguas,*" the man at the cart said.

Zip nodded. The man had put the five cups of ices into a cardboard container. Zip paid him, and then picked up the container with both hands. He kept frowning, and then the frown disappeared, and his face broke into a grin as he turned back toward the packing crate.

Frankie Hernandez had reached the hanging ladder of the fire escape.

Be careful with those bullets, he thought. *If you dumb bastards put them any lower, you'll hit me. And that would be the end of this little caper.*

Bracing himself, the gun in his holster now, he leaped up for the hanging ladder, missed, and dropped silently to the pavement. He flattened himself against the building and looked up. The volley from the rooftops was effectively keeping Miranda away from the windows. He moved out, jumped for the ladder again, caught it with one hand, reached up with the second hand, and then, hand over hand, began climbing. The ladder began to drop as he climbed, inching on squeaking, rusted iron hinges, drowned out by the roar of the guns from across the street. He drew his .38, hefted it in his hand, and began climbing the remaining rungs to the fire escape.

The people in the street watched him silently.

The guns showered destruction against the front of the building.

Zip was still smiling when he reached the crate, still thinking of what China had said. Somehow, he felt curiously relieved, as if ... as if something very heavy had been taken off his mind. And then he heard the voice.

"Well, now, ain't this nice? One of the darling Latin Purples bought ices for us!"

He looked up sharply. He recognized the gold jacket instantly, and the words "Royal Guardian" flashed into his mind, and he told himself not to be afraid, but he felt a tight knot of fear beginning in his stomach.

"H-hello, Tommy," he said.

"Hello, Zip," Tommy answered. "You're just in time. Get your boy off the box."

"Get ... but ..." He paused, nibbling his lip. The carton of ices in his hands felt suddenly very heavy. "But it's ... it's *my* box," he said. "I brought this all the way over from the ..."

"It belongs to whoever's using it," Tommy said. "And we want to use it."

"Aw look, Tommy," Zip said, "what do you want bad blood for, huh? Can't we ...?"

Tommy reached up suddenly, twisting his face into Papá's trouser leg, pulling him off balance, and dumping him into the street. Zip, his hands full of ices, his mind whirring with the new thoughts China had put there, stood by helplessly, wondering what to do now, wondering why ...

"Blow," Phil said to him.

"Aw, come on, Phil, can't we ...?"

"Li'l Killer," Phil corrected.

"Sure, can't we ...?"

"*Blow!*" Phil said firmly.

He shoved out at Zip suddenly. Tommy, trained for the maneuver, stuck out his foot. Zip tripped, staggered backward, the cups of ices leaving his hands and spattering over the street. He jumped to his feet instantly, his hand darting for his pocket. Nothing was in his mind right now but salvation. If China had said anything to him, he'd now forgotten it. All he knew was that he was being threatened by two Royal Guardians, that he was outnumbered and vulnerable.

As his hand closed on the switch knife in his pocket, he thought only *I got to get out of this*.

"Don't pull the blade, Zip," Tommy said gently.

Zip's eyes moved quickly to Tommy, saw that his hand was already in his pocket. They flicked to Phil who was ready to charge in on his flank. Undecided, he faced them. Elena, on the crate, began to laugh nervously. Tommy grinned and then picked up the laugh, and then Phil joined him, and their laughter was triumphant and, hearing the laughter, Zip began to tremble. He wanted to fight them, he wanted to destroy them, wanted to pull the blade and rip into them, show them who he was, show them who they were laughing at. But fear crawled in his belly like black worms, and he felt his fingers loosening their grip on the knife. In impotent rage, his eyes brimming with tears he did not wish to show, he whirled suddenly and kicked at one of the ices cups in the street.

And then he saw Hernandez on the fire escape.

Flat against the side of the building, edging silently past the first shattered window, and then the next, his gun in his hand, Hernandez hesitated for a moment, and then crouched beside the third window.

He brought up his revolver.

Zip understood what was happening in an instant.

Burning with shame and indignation, wanting to explode, wanting to show these rotten bastards they couldn't kick him around, wanting to shout, to rip, to gouge, to release the shame that growled inside him, wanting to show that he was Zip, Zip, ZIP!, he looked up at the first-floor windows and suddenly, without knowing why, he cupped his hands to his mouth.

"*Pepe!*" he bellowed. "*The fire escape!*"

13

When Hernandez heard the yell, he thought at first that his ears were deceiving him. His immediate reaction was to turn his head toward the street. And then he realized that Miranda, in the apartment, had whirled at the sound of the shouted words. And then he recognized the look in Miranda's eyes, and Hernandez tightened his finger on the trigger of the .38, and then he heard the explosions inside the apartment and then he was spinning backward and falling. He had been crouched outside the window, so he fell no more than three feet to the iron floor of the fire escape, but it seemed to him that he was falling through space for a very long time, and it seemed to him that he hit the iron slats with the force of a meteor slamming into the earth.

There were two bullets in his chest.

He had never been shot before, not when he'd been a Marine participating in the Iwo Jima landings, and not since he'd joined the police force. He had seen wounded men, a *lot* of wounded men, when he'd been in the service, but somehow he had detached the wound itself from the event which had caused the wound. He had been raised on the kid games of Cops and Robbers, Cowboys and Indians, *bang!* I got you! *bang!* you're dead! and there had always been something glamorous to the idea of getting shot. Even when he had seen the open gaping wounds, the notion of glamour had persisted.

He knew now that the notion was false, and he wondered which con man had ever sold him such a silly bill of goods. When the bullets slammed into his chest, he felt nothing at first but impact. He had been punched before, punched with hard driving fists that had knocked the wind out of him, and he knew what it felt like to be hit. He had once been struck with a hammer swung by a delirious building superintendent, catching the blow on his shoulder, feeling the sharp sudden pain of metal against flesh. But he had never been shot, and he knew now that when a man got shot he didn't daintily clutch his chest and say, "Uggggh!" and then do a fancy movie-extra dive. He knew that the force of a bullet was like the force of a steam locomotive, and he knew that when you got hit with a bullet, you got knocked off your feet. It was as simple as that. Maybe *everyone* didn't get knocked off his feet when he was shot, but the bullets that struck Hernandez spun him around from his crouch and then knocked him flat to the fire escape.

He felt only impact and shock at first, and then the cold sensation of falling through space, will-less, unable to control himself, simply falling, falling, and then colliding with metal, powerless to stick out his arms to cushion the fall.

And then he was on fire.

The fire engulfed him. It started with the two gaping holes in his back where the bullets had left his body, and then ran straight through his body like burning tunnels to the two smaller holes at the points of entry, and then suddenly flared up to consume his entire chest, and then his shoulders, and then his throat and his face, a roaring fire. He found it hard to breathe, he sucked in air through his parted lips, and he dimly realized that one of the bullets must have gone through a lung, and then blood bubbled out of his mouth, and he thought it was saliva until he saw its bright-red splash on the cuff of his shirt, and then he panicked.

Gasping for breath, his body on fire, pain lancing through him, he felt the panic rush into his head and settle behind his eyes like a pair of thumbs pressing outward. More blood bubbled from his mouth.

Giddily, he wondered if he were going to die.

The thumbs kept pressing against the backs of his eyes, spreading darkness which came in waves and retreated. He could hear shouting in the street below. He wondered if they'd collared whoever had done the yelling.

He wanted to puke.

He felt the nausea start deep in his stomach, tasted the vomit in his throat, and then the fire escape was spinning, the sky was spinning, the world was spinning, and he choked on his own blood and crashed into unconsciousness.

The boys had vanished like Arabian horse thieves.

Zip had begun running the moment he'd shouted the warning to Miranda, shoving his way through the crowd, dashing around the corner. Papá and Sixto, as soon as they realized what had happened, followed him. All three were gone before Byrnes, Carella, and Parker rushed from the doorway of the tenement.

Byrnes turned his head toward the fire escape instantly. "Frankie!" he yelled. "Frankie!" There was no answer.

"What happened?" Parker asked, struggling to catch his breath. "Is he dead?"

"I don't know. He's just laying up there. We got to get him down." He stared suddenly at the sidewalk beneath the fire escape. "What the hell is ... Jesus! Jesus Christ!"

"What is it?" Carella asked.

"That's blood!" Byrnes said, something like awe in his voice. "That's *blood* dripping down!"

The men watched the steady patter of drops to the pavement. The drops fell silently, as straight as arrows, one after the other, spattering to the pavement in an ever-widening stain.

"We got to get him off there," Byrnes said.

"It was a kid who yelled the warning to Miranda," one of the patrolmen said.

"Leave it to the kids," Byrnes said, shaking his head. "Sometimes I think the kids in this precinct are more damn trouble than all the professional thieves put together."

"It ain't them," Parker said, watching the dripping blood in fascination. "It's the parents. They come here without even knowing how to speak the language. What the hell can you expect?"

"My old man had a brogue you could cut with a knife," Byrnes said. "What's that got to do with..."

"What'd you say, Lieutenant?" a reporter behind the barricade asked. "About the kids?"

"Nothing for publication."

"You think the kids today will grow up to be like Pepe Miranda?"

"No. That's not what I think."

"What *do* you think, Lieutenant?"

"I think we've got a bleeding man on that fire escape, a man who may be dying. I think I want to get him off there while there's still a chance for him, and I think you'd better get off my back before I restrict the area to all reporters."

"Don't get touchy," the reporter said. "I've got to peg this story on *something*."

"On something? What the hell do you want? A Barnum and Bailey circus? Peg it on Miranda, peg it on Frankie Hernandez who may be up there dead, for all I know!"

"Life is cheap, Lieutenant," the reporter said.

"Is it? Then peg your story on your asshole! And leave me alone!" Angrily, Byrnes strode off toward the squad car.

"Boy," the reporter said, raising his eyebrows. "He's sure got a low boiling point, hasn't he?"

"He's been working in this precinct for a long time now," Parker said. "This ain't exactly the garden spot of the universe."

"I'm only trying to get some ideas about Miranda, that's all," the reporter said. "What the hell, nobody's job is easy."

"You want some ideas on Miranda?" Parker asked. "Then look around you. Miranda's only the end product. You don't have to be in that apartment with him to know what he's like. Just look around you, pal. You'll see Miranda in every stage of his development." Parker nodded sagely. "Just take a look," and then he followed Byrnes to the patrol car.

Tommy and Li'l Killer saw Cooch the moment he came around the corner.

"Hey, Tommy," Phil said. "There's one of them."

"One of who?"

"The Latin Purples. Man, if the cops spot that jacket..."

"Call him over," Tommy said.

"What for?"

"To tip him off. You want the cops to get him?"

"Who cares they get him or not? He's a jerk."

"Jerk or no, I don't like the cops to score. Call him over."

Phil shrugged. "Hey! Hey, kid! Hey, you!"

Cooch, who had been searching the crowd for Zip and the boys, stopped dead in his tracks, recognizing the gold jackets at once, hesitating.

"Come here," Phil said.

Cooch approached the crate warily. "You talking to me?"

"Yeah, Hey, what's your name again?"

"Me?"

"Yeah, who do you think? I forget your name. What is it again."

"Cooch."

"Sure. Cooch. That's right." Phil nodded. "Cooch, this is Tommy Ordiz, he's war counselor for the Royal Guardians. He's maybe got a tip for you."

"What kind of tip?" Cooch asked suspiciously.

"On the fourth at Hialeah," Phil said, and he burst out laughing.

"Don't clown around," Tommy warned. "You want this tip, Cooch?"

"Who's clowning?" Phil said. "Rrrrrrracing fans..."

"Knock it off!"

"I was just..."

"*Knock it off!*"

Phil fell silent. He put his hands in his pockets and glowered at Tommy.

"You want the tip, Cooch?" Tommy asked again.

"Depends on what kind."

"A good tip. I'm being nice to you." He paused. "Get rid of that purple jacket."

Cooch was silent for a moment. Then he said, "Who says?"

"I'm giving you good advice. Ditch the jacket."

"Why?" Cooch said narrowly. "So you can say you busted a Latin Purple?"

"Huh?"

"You heard me."

"Oh, man, don't be a worse meatball than you are," Tommy said. "I got better things to do than..."

"Screw him," Phil said. "Let him find out for himself."

"You don't get no trophy from me, pal," Cooch said.

"Look," Tommy started, patiently trying to explain, "if you keep wearing that jacket..."

"The jacket stays on! No goddamn Royal Guardian tells me what to wear."

"See?" Phil said. "What'd I tell you? Let the creep find out for . . ."

"No, wait a minute, Phil," Tommy said. Something hard and cold had crept into his voice and into his eyes. He studied Cooch minutely, and then said, "You ought to watch your mouth, boy, you know?"

"I don't have to watch nothing," Cooch said. He did not know whether or not he was afraid. Actually, he did not feel afraid. Not with four guns tucked into the waistband of his trousers. But at the same time, he knew that something was pushing him into sounding two members of the toughest gang in the neighborhood. He could only assume the force propelling him was fear. And yet, he did not feel afraid.

Tommy climbed down off the packing crate. "You got a *real* loose mouth, boy," he said. "You ought to watch the way it spills over."

"You take care of your own mouth," Cooch said.

"You're really looking for it, ain't you, boy? Your day ain't gonna be complete until we break your arm, is it?"

"You finished making big noises?" Cooch asked. "I'm in a hurry."

Tommy stepped into his path. "Stay put, boy."

"Tommy," Phil warned, "there's a million bulls all over the . . ."

"Shut up!" Tommy said tightly, without turning his attention from Cooch. "I give you a chance to take off that jacket nice and polite, now didn't I, Cooch? For your own good, I asked you. Okay. Now you're gonna take it off because I'm *telling* you to take it off. Now how about that?"

"How about it?" Cooch answered.

"You take it off, or I cut if off your back!"

"Sure. Try it."

"You're the kind I like," Tommy said, taking a step forward, his hand reaching into his pocket. "You're the kind of spunky little bastard I . . ."

"Hold it!" Cooch whispered. "Hold it right there, man! I got four pieces under this jacket, and I swear to God I'll use every friggin' one of them!"

Tommy stopped suddenly, eyeing Cooch, wondering if this were just a bluff. It did not seem to be. Cooch's eyes were steady, his mouth tight.

"So come on, hero," he said confidently.

"Let it go, Tommy," Phil said worriedly, his eyes flicking to the cops swarming over the street.

Tommy studied Cooch an instant longer, and then backed away. "We got a big man with a piece here, Phil," he said. "You're real big with them pieces, huh, Cooch? Well, I got some more advice for you. Friendly advice. Don't never go walking about without a piece from now on, you hear? Because, buddy, you are going to need one. You are really going to need one."

"Thanks, you yellow bastard," Cooch said, grinning, and then he turned on his heel and ran off toward the corner.

"Cooch, huh?" Tommy said, smoldering. He nodded. "Okay, Cooch. We're gonna see about you, Cooch."

"A nut!" Phil said, shaking his head. "We try to help him, and he turns on us." He shook his head again. "It just don't pay to be nice to nobody." He looked up at the girls. "You chicks gonna stand on that box all day long?"

"What else is there to do?" Elena asked.

"Let's go up to my pad," Phil said. "My people are out. We roll back the rug in the parlor, and we have a little jump, what do you say?"

"I don't know," Elena said. "Juana?"

"I don't know. What do you think?"

"It's too hot to dance," Elena said.

"Okay, so let's go get a beer," Phil said. "What the hell's the sense in hanging around here? Don't you know what's gonna happen?"

"No. What's gonna happen?"

"Eventually, they're gonna shoot Pepe," Phil said simply. "What do you think? He's gonna get away?"

"He might," Elena said.

"Impossible."

"Why is it so impossible?"

"Because there's got to be a moral," Phil said. "The Bad Guy never wins. Crime don't pay. Otherwise the Breen Office don't let it through." He burst out laughing. "Hey, Tommy, you dig that? The Breen Office..."

"Yeah, I caught it," Tommy said. "The son of a bitch! I was trying to help him, can you imagine that?"

"Come on, girls," Phil said. "Let's cut out, huh?"

"Juana?" Elena said.

"Okay," Juana said.

"Great," Phil said, helping them off the crate. "Believe me, you'd be wasting your time hanging around here. Ain't nothing gonna happen to Pepe but he's gonna get killed.

If the police had been as confidently sure of the outcome as was Phil, they would not have bothered to arm themselves with tear-gas pellets this time at the bat. For whatever Phil might have thought about the inevitability of Hollywood-type gangland movies, Pepe Miranda *had* broken out of an apartment the day before, and today he had shot a patrolman and a detective, and the possibility existed that he might shoot a few more detectives – or even another lowly patrolman or two – before the festivites were over. And, granting this possibility, there was the further possibility that he could and might break out of this apartment today, foiling the police, the Breen Office, the brothers Warner, and even Anthony Boucher.

In any case, this time the cops were playing it safe. One of their patrolmen had been carted away in an ambulance, and one of their detectives lay spilling his blood, drop by drop, to the sidewalk below, and those seemed like enough casualties for one day.

So they lined up across the street like Hessians on a Massachusetts field in 1777, and they put their tear-gas guns to their shoulders, and they awaited the order which would release a new volley of bullets against the windows across the street, driving Miranda back so that they could plop their triple tracer shells into the apartment. There was nothing as sad as a crying thief, and all those valiant men in blue would watch Miranda with aching hearts as he burst into tears, but that was the way the little tear-gas pellet bounced.

Lieutenant Byrnes waved his arm at the rooftops, and the volley began. There was no glass left to shatter, and even the window frames were so badly splintered that the new cascade of bullets seemed to seek out instinctively the relatively untouched brick surrounding the windows. Big chunks of red brick showered onto the fire escape and the pavement below. Hernandez, lying as still as a stone, was covered with red dust.

"Okay," Byrnes said to the men in the street, "get it going. Aim for the windows and get as many in there as you can!"

The men started firing. The triple tracer shells arced in lazy spirals toward the window. From inside the apartment, Miranda let out a roar like a wounded animal. There was a hiss, and then a cloud of smoke, and then more hisslike explosions and suddenly tear gas was pouring from the open windows. The pellets raced about the apartment like decapitated rats, designed to wriggle and squirm so that they could not be picked up and returned to the street. The scent of apple blossoms drifted into the street, a mild scent wafted over the heads of the crowd. Miranda was cursing a blue streak now, shouting and roaring. He appeared at the windows once, and was driven back by a Thompson gun which all but ripped away half the side of the building.

And then, suddenly, in the street, there was a pop and a hiss, and the scent of apple blossoms was unimaginably strong, and Andy Parker reeled backward from one of the patrolmen and shouted, "You stupid idiot! You goddamn stupid idiot!"

14

Well, you can't blame people for accidents. People have accidents all the time, and cops are only people, and if a gun misfires, it misfires, and that's that. And if a tear-gas pellet which is supposed to go zooming up through the air suddenly plops onto the asphalt and explodes there, those are just the breaks. Maybe Parker shouldn't have been standing so close to the patrolman firing the pellet. But accidents *will* happen, and Parker *was* standing close to the gun when it misfired, and close to the pellet when it exploded, so that he got the first mushrooming whiff of tear gas before the pellet went dizzily skipping into the crowd. Tear gas ain't Chanel Number 5. Especially when it goes off practically in your face. His eyes began to burn instantly. Blindly, he reached for his handkerchief, cursing the patrolman, and compounding the felony by rubbing the chemical deeper into his smarting eyes.

Bawling like a baby, he staggered toward the luncheonette, the handkerchief to his face. Behind him he could hear the shrieking of the crowd as the pellet traced a crazy path among them. People began coughing and shouting. Byrnes was yelling orders at patrolmen. All Parker knew was that his face and his eyes were burning.

"Luís!" he shouted. "Luís!"

He groped his way to the counter, the handkerchief to his face.

"Luís, where are you?"

There was no answer. Parker took the handkerchief away from his face. He tried to see past the tears in his eyes, but he saw only blurred shapes, dazzling, shimmering tears of streaked light.

"Luís!" he shouted. "Get me some water! I can't see." He was beginning to panic. Why didn't Luís answer him? Why wouldn't Luís help him? "Luís! *Where are you?* Help me! Get me some water! *Luís! Luís!*"

Luís came running from the back of the shop, his eyes wide with concern. "*Qué pasa?*" he said. "*Qué pasa?*"

And Parker shouted. "Where are you, you stupid spic!"

The words stopped Luís as effectively as bullets. They slammed into his ears and ricocheted in his mind and then paralyzed him. He stood with his arms at his sides, staring at Parker.

"Luís?"

"*Sí.*"

"For Christ's sake, get me some water. Please get me some water."

"*Sí,*" Luís said. "*Sí.*" Dazed, he moved away from the counter.

"Hurry!"

In the street outside, the firing had stopped. Great billows of gas poured from the shattered windows of the apartment, hovered on the windless air. People were covering their faces with handkerchiefs and cursing at the police for unleashing this blight. Luís brought a bowl of water to the counter. Parker groped for it blindly, touched the rim with his hand, and then dipped into it. Luís watched him silently. Parker washed his eyes and his skin, sighing, repeating the motion over and over again. And finally he dried himself with the handkerchief and lifted his face. Luís was still staring at him.

"*Qué pasa, maricón?*" Parker asked, grinning, using a Spanish obscenity.

"Nothing," Luís said. He shook his head wearily. "Nothing."

"What's the matter, huh?" Parker asked, still grinning. "What's the matter, eh, *cabrón?*" Another obscenity, but there was no answering smile from Luís.

"*De nada,*" Luís said. "Nothing."

"You sore at me? 'Cause I was yelling at you? Is that it? Man, I felt like my eyes were on fire. You sure were a lifesaver."

"*Sí*, I was a lifesaver," Luís said blankly.

Parker felt suddenly uneasy. "Hey, come on," he said. "You going to let a little yelling come between friends?"

After a long while, Luís said, "No, Andy, I would not let a little yelling come between friends."

Outside, Lieutenant Byrnes lifted the megaphone to his lips. "*Miranda? Can you hear me?*"

"What do you want, you son of a bitch?" Miranda shouted, coughing.

"*This is it, Miranda. Are you ready to come out? Or do we shoot our way in?*"

There was a long silence. Parker moved quickly out of the luncheonette. Luís was still staring at him as he left.

"What the hell is he doing?" Parker asked Carella. "Why don't we move in right now? I'll bet he can hardly see in there."

"Pete doesn't want any more shooting unless it's absolutely necessary," Carella answered.

"Why give that punk a break? We can go in there and mop him up in two seconds."

"Suppose he starts shooting into the street again?"

"So what?"

"You want these people to get hurt?"

"All I want is Miranda."

"And after Miranda, then what?" Carella asked.

"What do you mean?"

"When does your private crusade stop?"

"What the hell are you...?"

"When are you going to forget that beating you took, Parker?"

"What beating? What...?"

"You know what I'm talking about!"

"All right. I'm never going to forget it," Parker shouted. "Okay? Never. It taught me a lesson, buddy, and only a sap would..."

"What lesson, Parker?"

"It taught me you can't trust anybody in this lousy precinct, that's what it..."

"And it also taught you to be afraid," Carella said.

"What?"

"You heard me. Afraid."

"Look, mister, you'd just better stop right now, while you're winning. I still ain't forgotten the time you..."

"When are you going to make a *real* arrest, Parker? When are you going to stop pulling in junkies and drunks? When are you going to tackle the real troublemakers?"

"I do my job!" Parker shouted. "I keep the streets clean!"

"By picking up the wrong garbage!"

"It's *all* garbage here!"

"And you're afraid of it! You're afraid to take another beating!"

"You son of a bitch, I warned you to..."

"*I'm waiting, Miranda!*" Byrnes shouted, and both men turned their attention to the lieutenant. Carella's fists were bunched. Parker glowered at him, and then walked to where Byrnes was standing.

"How about it, Miranda? Give it up! You haven't got a chance."

"What chance do I have if I come out? That old lady died, didn't she?"

"What old lady?"

"The one I mugged," Miranda said. He went into a fit of coughing which lasted for several moments. Then his voice came from the apartment again. "Tell the truth, cop."

"That woman's still alive, Miranda."

"I shouldn't have hit her," Miranda said. His voice faded. "I needed money. I had to..." He paused for a long time. "She's dead, ain't she?"

"She's alive, I told you."

"You're lying to me. You'll never get me out of here, cop. You think I'm coming out to face a murder rap?"

"The woman's alive. If you force us to come in after you, you haven't got a chance."

"I got news for you, cop. I never *did* have one."

"Okay, so make it easy on yourself now."

"For what? In payment for all the crap I've taken from cops since I was old enough to walk?"

"You dished out a bit yourself, Miranda. Let's cut the talking. Yes or no? Do you come out with your hands up, or do we blast you out?"

"You want me, come and earn your salary."

"Okay, you're calling it. There's just no talking to you, is there? Okay, we're coming in."

"Hey ... hey, cop!"

"What is it?"

"Listen, I ... I want a priest."

"A what?"

"A priest. I ... I wanna talk to a priest."

"Will you come out if we get you one?"

"Send him up here. I gotta talk to him."

"Why? Are you hit?"

"No, I ain't hit. Goddamnit, do I need a federal warrant to get a priest? Can't I get anything in this friggin' city without having to beg for it?"

"*Just a minute, Miranda.*" Byrnes put down the megaphone. "What do you think, Steve?"

"It's a trick," Carella said.

"Sure," Parker said. "He don't want no priest. All he wants is a shield."

"I know," Byrnes said.

Carella stared at him. "Are you thinking what I'm thinking, Pete?"

"Yes," Byrnes said. He put the speaker to his mouth. "*Miranda?*"

"Yeah?"

"*I'm getting a priest for you.*"

There was something in Zip's eyes which had not been there before. Sixto studied his face and tried to figure out what it was. Zip looked as if he might begin crying at any moment. His face was red, and his lips were tight, and his eyes seemed to blink too often, as if he were struggling to hold back tears. But at the same time, there was a strength to the rigid thrust of his back, an impatience to the way he clenched and unclenched his fists.

The boys were standing on the avenue opposite Alfredo's building. None of them wore the purple jackets now. Without the jackets, they seemed like four high-school kids discussing girls or baseball or swimming. But, of course, they were discussing murder.

"What do you think, Cooch? Is he up there or not?"

"I don't know," Cooch said, looking across at the building. "One thing for sure, he didn't go to church."

"Why we deetch dee jackets, hey?" Papá asked. "I lak dee purple jacket."

"The jackets are hot," Zip said impatiently. "Can't you keep your mind on what we're doing here?"

"But I lak dee jacket. I don't see why . . ."

"You think this is the right time, Zip?" Cooch interrupted. "The streets are crawling with bulls."

"It's *exactly* the right time. Every cop in the city's got his hands full with Pepe. We can move in on Alfie and get him before they even know what happened."

"What's dee sense havin' a jacket if you cann wear it, huh?" Papá persisted.

Zip whirled on him angrily. For a moment, it seemed as if he would strike him. "You want to end up on Bailey's Island?" he shouted.

"Where's dat?"

"In the middle of the River Dix! It's a prison. You wear the jacket, and that's where you'll wind up."

"Wha' did I do, huh?" Papá asked. "Why I cann wear dee jacket? Why they put me in jail if I wear dee jacket?"

"Oh, man, try to explain anything to this moron! Why the hell don't you go back where you came from?" Zip said angrily. "Go to Puerto Rico, will ya? Do me a favor."

"If I b'long dee Latin Purples," Papá said logically, unfazed, "I shoul' wear dee jacket. Den ever'body knows who I am. Thass what you say, Zeep. So now I cann wear dee jacket. Why not?"

"Don't try to figure it out, Papá," Zip said. "Just take my word for it. Right now, we got Alfie to worry about."

"Cann we let it wait, Zip?" Sixto said. "Wha's the hurry? Maybe tomorrow . . ."

Zip's eyes flashed, and again he looked as if he were about to cry, and yet he seemed strong and determined at the same time. "Now!" he said. "Today! I'm sick of waiting for tomorrow! I'm gonna be somebody *today!*"

"You don' have to kill Alfie to be somebody," Sixto said.

"What's the sense talking to a tiger? You're like a goddamn foreigner. Look we ain't debating this no more. It's decided already."

"But who decided?" Sixto asked.

"*I* decided."

"Then why don' *you* go shoot him?"

The words came out of his mouth before he realized he was going to say them. They produced an instant silence. Zip clenched his fists and then unclenched them.

"What's your story, Sixto?" he said softly.

Sixto took a deep breath. "I don' think we should shoot him."

"You don't, huh?"

"No."

"Well, I think we should. And that's that."

"That's what . . ."

"That's *what?*" Zip said, his fists working. "Go ahead, finish it."

"Tha's what Pepe Miranda would do," Sixto blurted. "Tha's not what my fodder would do. My fodder woul'n shoot nobody."

"So what the hell is your father? A big shot? He works in a factory, for Pete's sake!"

"What's wrong wi' workin' in a factory?"

"You want to be a factory worker, go ahead. I don't wanna work in no damn factory!"

"What you *wanna* do?" Sixto asked, and again there was a silence. He was certain that Zip would begin crying this time. This time the tears seemed on the verge of eruption. "You wanna go aroun' killing people all the time? Is that what you wanna do?" Sixto persisted.

"Look . . ."

"You tink it's so smart to kill somebody? My people never kill nobody, not here, not on the islan'. So what's so special abou' . . ."

"You're looking for trouble," Zip said quietly.

"We kill Alfie . . . wha's the sense? What does that make us?"

"You're looking for trouble," Zip repeated.

"You tink 'cause we beat up somebody, 'cause we ..."

"Shut up!"

"... act like tough guys ..."

Zip slapped him suddenly and viciously. Sixto's head snapped back. He was shocked for a moment, and the blow had hurt him. But he stared at Zip coldly, and then wiped his hand across his mouth.

"All right?" Zip asked.

Sixto did not answer. Cooch watched his face, a slight smirk beginning on his mouth. Papá seemed confused, as if he did not know whether to smile or frown.

"All right?" Zip asked again. Again, there was no answer. "All right," he said nodding. "Let's map this out."

Cooch grinned. He was glad this nasty disciplinary business was out of the way. He was glad they were moving into action again. "What's the first step, Zip?"

"First, we gotta find out if Alfie's still in the apartment. Papá, you and Sixto'll take care of that. Go up in the hallway and listen outside the door. If he's in there, you'll hear him. Then you come back and report to me."

"How do we get him out, Zip?" Cooch asked.

"All we got to do is get him in the hallway."

"But how?"

"I don't know." He paused, thinking. "Ain't he got no buddies? Like Papá could call him out, makin' believe he was a buddy."

Cooch shook his head. "Alfie's a lone wolf."

"There must be somebody he trusts, somebody he'd come out in the hallway to talk ... hey!" He snapped his fingers. His face was suddenly alive. If ever he'd looked about to cry, he did not look that way now. "Sure," he said. "We say we want to be friends, see? That's the story we give. And the go-between believes it, and tells that to Alfie. When Alfie comes out in the hallway, *bam!*"

"Yeah, but who, Zip? Who's gonna be the go-between? Who we gonna get that Alfie would trust?"

Zip grinned from ear to ear.

"China," he said.

15

In the hallway of the building in which Alfredo Gomez lived, Sixto suddenly knew what had to be done. Perhaps he had known it all along, perhaps he had known ever since he'd gone into the drugstore, known without admitting it to himself. But he knew now that one could not stand committed by refusing to commit oneself. And he knew now that more than the mere presence of police on the street was necessary to prevent the senseless murder of Alfredo Gomez. He recognized that he must choose a side and choose it now, and that once he had made his choice he would have to defend it. He was very young to be finding himself at such a crossroad. Too young, perhaps, to be making a choice which would influence another's life as well as his own. But the crossroad was there, and he faced it, and he made his choice unheroically. He made his choice the way most choices are made, made it through a combination of character and conviction. For Sixto, no other choice would have been possible. The choice was as much a part of him as his hands.

"Papá," he whispered.

'Wha's dee matter?" Papá said.

"Sit down. I wann to talk to you."

The boys sat on the steps leading to the first floor. It was dark in the hallway, and quiet. Most of the building's tenants were out in the street watching the siege. But even though he knew he would not be overheard, Sixto whispered. And because whispering is contagious, Papá whispered, too. Side by side in the darkened hallway, the boys talked.

"Wha's dee matter?" Papá asked again.

"Papá ... this ... this is all wrong."

"Wha's all wronn?"

"What we going to do. To Alfie."

"Zeep say ..."

"Papá, please. Listen to me. Please."

"I lis'nin', Sixto."

"Iss wrong to kill Alfie, Papá."

"Wronn? But Zeep say ..."

"Iss wrong! Papá, look ... look, you like it here? You like this city?"

"*Sí.*"

"We come here ... is nice here ... is better. We don' want to be like that Pepe Miranda up there!"

Papá hesitated for a moment, confused. Then he said, "Pepe Miranda's the grays thin' ever happen this neighborhood."

"No, Papá. No. He brings shame to us."

Papá shook his head. Gently, like a father about to explain something to a favored child, he covered Sixto's hand with his own. Then, with little patting motions characteristic of the slow movement which had earned him his nickname, he said, "No, no *you* wronn, Sixto. He the grays thin' ever happen aroun' here."

"Papá, he *kills* people!" Sixto said, pulling back his hand.

"*Sí.* He's brave."

"Papá, that's not ..."

"He's a brave man," Papá insisted. "He hole off all dee cops, an' he . . ."

"He's not brave! He's no good! He don' care for you or me, ony for himself. He iss bad, an' he brings disgrace to us."

"No, Sixto," Papá said slowly. "*No es verdad. De ningún modo . . .*"

"Don' speak Spanish!" Sixto said. "We here now, we speak English." He paused. "Papá, you understan' what I'm saying?"

"*Sí, yo comprendo. Pero . . .*"

"Don' speak Spanish!"

"Why I cann speak Spanish?" Papá asked, puzzled.

"Papá, listen to me," Sixto said desperately. "We not gonna kill Alfie."

"Sure, we gon' kill him," Papá said, nodding.

"No. No, we not. We kill him, then we doin' wrong. Like Zip. Like Pepe."

"Zeep bought me *pidaguas*, Sixto," Papá said.

"Papá, he iss bad."

"Zeep? Bad?"

"Yes, yes."

"An' Pepe?"

"Yes, him too."

"No," Papá said. He shook his head. "Zeep say he iss good."

Sixto was trembling. He did not want to play his trump, and yet he saw that Papá was still unconvinced, saw that more was needed.

"Papá, you think I am good?"

"*Sí.*"

"Would I do something bad, Papá?"

"No. I don' think so."

"Papá . . ."

He sucked in a deep breath.

"Papá . . . the one who called the police . . . the one who

told them where Pepe wass ... it was me. I called them."

The hallway was silent. He felt at once that he had made a terrible mistake, that he had revealed something which should have remained secret. Papá studied him with blank eyes.

"*You* tole on Pepe?" he asked incredulously.

"Yes."

"How you know where he wass?"

"I saw him yesterday. I recognize his picture from the paper. All day, I wonder about it. Then I think ... I think it's best to tell."

"But ... but tha's bein' ... a *rat*, Sixto."

"No."

"But you tole on Pepe!"

"Yes."

"Why? Why you do this?"

"Because he iss bad."

Papá was silent for a long time. Then he scratched his head and said, "If Pepe iss bad, why does Zeep say...?"

"Zip only wants to be big. He thinks it makes him big to boss. But it's ony big when you let everybody live his own life. Papá, listen. Please. Please listen." He suddenly felt like crying. He clutched Papá's arm fiercely and said, "Papá, we go this way now, we never stop, you hear?"

"I hear. *Sí, sí.*"

"We go this way now, we get like Zip, and then we wind up like Pepe. We bring more shame to the *barrio*. We hurt ourselves."

"*Sí, sí, comprendo.*"

"*Papá, quien adna al revés anda el camino dos veces.* If we take the wrong road, we make the journey twice."

"But ... Zeep iss *bad*?"

"Yes, yes."

Struggling with this new idea, Papá said, "But he bought me *pidaguas*," and then fell silent. His brow was furrowed, his eyes puzzled. After a long time, he said, "An' Pepe iss bad too?"

"Yes."

"Sixto ... iss you alone who thinks like this? Or ever'body?"

"Everybody, Papá. Everybody in the streets."

"I ... Sixto ... I wanna be lak ever'body in thees city. But Zeep say ..."

"Papá, we are only strong if we do the right thing."

Again, Papá was silent, thinking. He shrugged and turned to Sixto.

"I ... I don' wann to be dee bad guy, Sixto."

"No."

"I wann to be dee goo' guy."

"*Sí, sí.*"

He shrugged again. "I don' know how to say in English."

"You are with me, Papá?"

Papá beamed. "*Sí,* I am wi' you, Sixto." He continued smiling. "Sixto?" He paused. "We dee goo' guys, Sixto?"

"Yes, Papá," Sixto said very softly. "We the good guys."

The other good guys came up the street.

There were two of them. One was a detective lieutenant named Peter Byrnes. The other was a priest named Steve Carella.

Carella felt rather foolish. He had felt foolish in the rectory of the church while arguing with Father Donovan who had, perhaps rightfully, insisted that the policemen were planning something which would make a mockery of a man's faith in God.

"This man doesn't have a faith in God," Byrnes had said. "He wants a priest up there for one reason and one reason alone. He wants to use him as a shield to get out of that apartment."

"How do you know that?"

"I know it," Byrnes said. "Take my word for it. The last time Pepe Miranda was inside a church was the day he was baptized."

"He may wish to make his peace."

"Father, I respect your attitude, believe me. But I think I know a little more about this man than you do. Now you can either let me borrow one of your black things, whatever you call them..."

"Cassock."

"Yes, your cassock, or else we'll have to root around someplace else and find one. That'll take time, and Miranda may shoot somebody else during that time. Now, it's up to you."

"And suppose his request for a priest is legitimate?" Father Donovan asked.

"Then I'll come straight down from the apartment, and I'll come straight here, and I'll give you back your hassock..."

"Cassock."

"Cassock, and you can go up and see him yourself. Is that fair?"

"It sounds fair." Father Donovan had studied Byrnes. "My garment would never fit you, Lieutenant."

"I'll squeeze into it."

Father Donovan shook his head. "No. You've got at least thirty pounds on me. The garment is cut tight to begin with."

"Father, we're in an awful hurry. Could we please...?"

"Besides," Carella said, "you can't go up there, Pete."

"Why not?"

"You've been our talk-man so far. If somebody else starts using the megaphone, Miranda'll get suspicious. You've got to stay in the street and keep talking to him."

"I'm going up," Byrnes said. "I wouldn't ask any of my men to take a chance like..."

"The cassock doesn't fit you," Carella said.

"The hell with the ... pardon me, Father."

"And Miranda would smell a rat," Carella said.

"I don't care what he..."

"So I'd better go up. Father Donovan and I are about the same size."

"Steve, you can't..."

"That's settled," Carella said.

"Steve..."

"What?"

"I ... nothing." He paused. "He's a killer."

"I know."

"And it was *my* idea to..."

"It was *our* idea. We got it at the same time, Pete. Remember?"

"If you get shot, you damn fool..."

"I've been shot before," Carella said.

The men stared at each other.

"All right," Byrnes said, sighing, "where's the cassock, Father?"

Now, walking down the street, Carella still felt foolish. For if Pepe Miranda had not been inside a church since the day of his baptism, Carella hadn't been inside one – not to pray, at least – since shortly after his confirmation. That was a long, long time ago. Parading down the street now in a priest's long black apparel, feeling the cold hard snout of a .38 against his belly beneath the black cloth, trying to look pious as hell, he felt only foolish. A set of prayer beads was entwined around his right hand. He quickly shifted them to his left, so that his right would be free for a quick draw if it came to that.

"What's the plan?" he asked Byrnes.

"I'll tell Miranda we've got his priest. He'll probably check from the window. Then you go up."

"Then what?"

"If he wants to confess or something, let him confess. Watch for your chance, and slug him if he turns his back."

"But you told Father Donovan..."

"Yeah, I lied in church," Byrnes said. "Actually, Miranda isn't going to make any confession, Steve. He's going to grab you the minute you walk into that apartment, and he's going to use you as a shield when he walks out."

"What do I do? Wait for my chance and then..."

"You do nothing. Let him lead you out. I'll have men on either side of the doorway. The minute he steps into the street, you'd better duck." Byrnes paused. "I'd feel a lot happier if I were doing this myself, Steve."

"Why?" Carella grinned. "Because I might get killed? My goodness, what a thing to be worrying about."

"You're not worried about it, huh?"

"Didn't you hear that reporter, Pete?"

"What do you mean?"

"Life is cheap," Carella answered.

They had come up to the squad car now. Byrnes reached into it for the megaphone. "You set, Steve?"

"As set as I'll ever be."

"Steve, we're going to begin blasting the minute he clears the front stoop. The shots will be coming from behind him, but I can't guarantee that all these bums learned anything at the police academy. When you clear the stoop, make a dive for the sidewalk."

"Okay."

"Good luck."

"Thanks." Carella paused. "Suppose he just wants to pray a little?"

Byrnes shrugged. "You've got a set of prayer beads. Use them." He paused. "Good luck," he said again.

"Let's get it moving," Carella said, "before I chicken out."

Byrnes picked up the megaphone and blew into it. "*Miranda?*" he called. There was no answer. "*Miranda?*" Still no answer.

"Maybe he slit his own throat," Carella whispered.

"*Miranda, this is Lieutenant Byrnes. Can you hear me?*"

"I hear you. What is it?"

"*We've got your priest.*"

"Where is he? Get him out in the middle of the street. I want to see him."

Carella nodded at Byrnes, and then took a deep breath. Slowly, he walked to the center of the street.

"*You can't see him if you don't look,*" Byrnes said.

There was a long silence. Suddenly, Miranda's head popped up above the window sill. He looked into the street for no longer than ten seconds, and then dropped from sight again. Even in that short a time, Byrnes and Carella saw that his eyes were puffed and his face was streaked.

"All right," Miranda shouted. "Send him up."

"*Not so fast, Miranda,*" Byrnes said, thinking, I've got to make this look good. He knows we wouldn't send up a priest unless he makes some concession. He knows we're considering the idea that this may be a trap. He knows we're not stupid.

"What is it now?" Miranda said.

"*The priest stays right where he is unless I get some promises from you,*" Byrnes said.

"Here we go," Miranda answered, and the people in the street began chuckling.

"*Yes, here we go, Miranda. I'm not sending up a man you can use as a shield to get out of that apartment.*"

"What kind of a louse do you think I am?"

"*Do I have to answer that one?*" Byrnes said, and again the crowd chuckled. This was beginning to get good. None of that grim stuff any more. Just a plain old battle of wits, like a good television routine.

"All right, cop, what do you want from me?"

"*Number one: we're sending up an unarmed man who insists he wants to see you alone as a representative of God. I want you to respect that, Miranda.*" God forgive me, Byrnes thought.

"All right, all right."

"*Number two: I want you to talk to him. About coming out of there. I don't know why you want to see him, and I don't care. But I want your promise that you'll talk to him about coming out.*"

"Is that all?"

"*Do I have your promise?*"

"What makes you think I'll keep any promise I make?"

"*This is a man of God, Miranda.*"

"Okay, okay, I promise."

"*Did you hear him, Father?*" Byrnes asked Carella.

"I heard him," Carella answered.

"*You can enter the building any time you like.*"

Carella nodded, sucked in another deep breath, walked directly to the front stoop of the tenement, and entered the hallway.

Byrnes put down the megaphone, looked at his watch, and then told Captain Frick he wanted four of the best marksmen he could find. Then he began praying.

16

If you're God, you've got all these little things to take care of, you see. Oh, not the business of getting the sun to rise on time, or the stars to come out. And not riding herd on the seasons so that they arrive when they're supposed to, not things like that. Those are the big things, and the big things almost take care of themselves. It's those damn *little* things that get so bothersome. And if you're God, you can't just ignore them, you know. You can, of course, move in mysterious ways your wonders to perform. This means that you can leave a few loose ends here and there and nobody will question them because you are, after all, God. Maybe you've got a bigger design in mind which will not become apparent to us poor slobs until maybe decades from now. Or centuries. So who are we to question? Being God, you are perfectly entitled to occasional sloppiness.

Or maybe these things aren't even in your control, who knows? Maybe you just sort of set the universe every day, the way somebody sets a clock, and then let it run on its own, fast or slow, however it wants to, without touching it again until it's run down and needs another winding. Maybe that's the way you operate, and nobody's going to question that either, God, you can bet your life on that, God.

Only sometimes, no offense meant, you ought to work a thing out and not just let it happen, you know? Like take that Puerto Rican girl and that sailor, take them for example. Now, being God, you could fix them up real fine, couldn't you? Like, for example, Zip and Cooch could find her, you see, and Zip is dragging her down the street towards Alfie's pad when *wham!* who should appear? The sailor! How's that, huh? He didn't go off with the whore Marge, you see. He only started to, but then he changed his mind. And here he is back on the street, face to face with China. He looks at her, and she looks at him, and their eyes lock, and slowly they walk across that street to each other, and tolerance and understanding flash in the sailor's eyes, *I love you, China,* coupled with a little bit of honest lust, *I love you, Jeff, wham* they clinch, and we fade out on Zip who shrugs his shoulders and says, "Oh well, what the hell, easy come, easy go."

How's that, God?

That's great.

But that isn't the way it happened.

The street was impossible. The crowd was anxious for the kill now, anxious for the die to be cast either way. They didn't much give a damn at this moment whether or not Miranda would kill the priest and the police lieutenant and the commissioner and the mayor and the governor and even the president. They didn't care whether or not a cop on one of the rooftops would fire a lucky shot and catch Miranda *splank* between the eyeballs. They only wanted it to be over and done with, either way. And so the crowd was restless, and a little mean, and hot, and uncomfortable. It was a crowd which was beginning to resent this tie game which had run into fourteen innings. The tenth inning had been a treat and the eleventh a distinct bonus and the twelfth a lovely dividend, but the thirteenth brought on thoughts of other things to be done. Watching a game was great fun – but life was real and life was earnest, and life was going on *outside* that ball park.

So the crowd resisted the shoving of Zip and Cooch, and occasionally the crowd shoved back at the two boys and cursed a bit, and did everything possible to make the task of locating China unimaginably difficult.

In fifteen minutes' time, Zip and Cooch gave up the search.

It was just as well that they had, because China wasn't in the neighborhood any longer. China had gone over to the park where she had sat by the lake and watched the people in the rowboats. That's where China was. She cried a little, yes. In the park, by the lake, watching the rowboats.

The sailor? Did he wander back to the street? Did he amble over to the park?

The sailor went to bed with a prostitute named Marge. Marge was a practiced whore, and she pleased the sailor immensely. The sailor paid her fifteen dollars, which was nearly every cent he had. Then he walked to the subway, got on a train, went downtown to where his ship was docked, started up the gangway, saluted the ensign on the fantail, saluted the officer of the deck, went to the rear compartment, took off his whites, put on a pair of dungarees and a chambray shirt, climbed into his sack, and went to sleep until the loud-speaker amidships announced, "Chow down." He ate a good dinner, saw a movie on the boat deck that evening, went to bed about eleven o'clock, and sailed for San Diego the next morning. He never saw the Puerto Rican girl named China again in his life. He probably went back to Fletcher, Colorado, eventually. Maybe she flashed into his mind every now and then – like once every twelve years. Maybe he remembered her dimly and wondered what had become of her. Maybe, married to Corrine and running an insurance business, he sporadically thought of China in an idealized way, the most beautiful girl in the world, exotic, that day in a strange city, far away, I wonder what became of her, I wonder.

She sat in the park and wept a bit and watched the rowboats.

You are God, and you can do it any way you want to. You can even get them married the next day before his ship sails. Anything you want to do. All the possibilities are there. And you're God, and there isn't anyone who's going to slap your wrist, no matter how you do it.

But God, man, that is the way it happened.

Steve Carella knocked on the door. There were bullet holes in the door, and Carella remembered that Pepe Miranda had shot a patrolman through that door, and he suddenly wanted his .38 in his hand.

Now, easy, he told himself. Now just take it easy, and don't panic. We are going to play this Miranda's way because there are a lot of people out there on the street, and we don't want them to be getting shot. So be cool. Your hand is shaking, and you are itching to pull that .38 so that you'll have something more than a set of prayer beads in your fist when that door opens, but be cool, Steve-o, be cool and . . .

The door opened.

A .45 automatic was the first thing Carella saw. The door opened just a crack, and there was the .45, its big ugly snout pointing into the hallway. Carella's mouth felt very dry.

"I'm . . . Father Donovan," he said to the automatic.

The door opened wider. Carella's eyes panned up from the .45, the hand holding it, the thin wrist, the black hair curling on the arm, the narrow shoulders, the sweat-stained undershirt, the sudden puff of black hair in the hollow of the throat, the wings of the man's collarbones, his thin neck, and high cheekbones, brown eyes, puffed lids, a balding head, and desperation. Add a man up, add the parts, form a total picture, and the total is desperation. It was there in

Miranda's eyes and in his mouth and even in the way he held the .45, his head tilted to one side, his shoulder sort of leaning into the gun, the gun close to his body as if it were something he cherished, a tie to reality.

"Come in a minute," Miranda said.

Carella stepped into the apartment. The place was a shambles. The furniture, the floors, everything in the room bore the ravaging marks of gunfire. It was inconceivable to think that a human being had been in this bullet-pocked room and managed to escape getting shot.

"Looks like they dropped an atom bomb in here, don't it?" Miranda said.

"Yes," Carella answered.

"You're not scared, are you? They won't shoot with you in here, it's all right."

Carella nodded. He was not scared. It was only ... he felt odd all at once. He did not feel like a cop. Miranda was not treating him as if he were a cop. Miranda was behaving as if he were truly a priest, a person he could talk to, relax with. He wanted to say, "I'm not what you think, Miranda! Don't show yourself to me!" but the words would not come.

"Boy, this has been murder," Miranda said. "Look, I didn't ask you up here to confess to you or nothing. I think we ought to get that straight."

"Then why did you ask me to come up?"

"Well..." Miranda shrugged. He seemed like a young kid in that moment, a young kid who is about to tell a priest that he took off a girl's underpants on the roof. Carella kept staring at him. Miranda held the .45 in his hand loosely, expecting no trouble from this man he thought was a priest, embarrassed because he was about to reveal something, dishonorable to him. "I'll put it to you straight, Father," he said. "I got to get out of this apartment."

"Yes?"

"So ... so you're going to take me out."

"I am?"

Miranda nodded. "I know that's pretty crumby. But I got to get out of here."

"Where do you go from here, Pepe?"

"I don't know." Miranda shook his head. "You know, Father, you reach the point where ... where there ain't many places left to go." He laughed nervously. "Where..." He laughed again. "I don't know. I don't know where I'll go once I get out of here."

"There're a lot of cops out there, Pepe."

"Yeah, I know." He sighed. "Man, this kind of stuff ... I *hate* this kind of Public Enemy Number One stuff, you dig? I just hate it. Oh man, it's like ... like something is expected of me, you know what I mean? I've *got* to be the bad guy. I don't know if it makes any sense to you, Father."

"I'm not sure it does," Carella answered, puzzled.

"Well, like ... like there are sides. I'm the bad guy." He shrugged. "I've *always* been the bad guy. Ever since I was a kid. So I'm still the bad guy. They expect me to be the bad guy. The people, I mean. It's like ... I don't know if I can explain this. It's like sometimes I don't know who is the real Pepe Miranda, and who is the guy I ... the *pictures* of the guy, you follow? The various *pictures* of the guy."

"I don't know what you mean," Carella said.

"The *pictures*," Miranda repeated. "Like the cops have a picture of me." He chuckled. "It's got a number right across the face of it." He chuckled again. "And the people in the street got another picture of me. And the kids got a picture. And *you* got a picture. But they're all different pictures, and none of them are really me, Pepe Miranda."

"Then who is?" Carella asked.

"I don't know."

"You've killed people, Pepe."

"Yeah." He paused. "I know." He shrugged, but it was not a shrug of indifference, not a shrug which said, "So I killed people, so what?" If it had been that, Carella would have instantly felt like a cop again. But it was not that. It was simply a shrug which said, "I know I've killed people, but I don't know why," and so Carella still felt like a man who had come up here to *talk* to Miranda, not to harm him.

"Well, anyway," Miranda said, "I've got to get out of here."

"Because the people in the street expect it?" Carella asked.

"No. No, I don't think that's..."

"Then why?"

"Well..." Miranda sighed heavily. "I ain't got a chance, Father," he said simply.

"Then give up."

"Why? Go to jail? Maybe the electric chair if that woman dies? Don't you see? I got nothing to lose."

He recognized in an instant that Miranda was absolutely right. Moreover, if Carella were in his position, in this apartment, surrounded by policemen, facing either a lifelong jail sentence or death in the electric chair, he would undoubtedly react in exactly the way that Miranda was reacting. He would try to get out of that apartment by fair means or foul. He would try to escape.

"Well..." he said, and he fell silent.

The two men faced each other.

"You see what I mean, Father?"

"Well..."

Miranda shrugged. The apartment was silent.

"So ... so I got to use you as a shield, Father. They won't shoot if I come out with you in front of me."

"Suppose they refuse to recognize..."

"Oh, they won't. They won't try nothing. I'll tell them I'll shoot you if they try anything."

"And if they *should* try something? *Will* you shoot me, Pepe?"

Pepe Miranda frowned.

"*Will* you, Pepe?"

After a long while he said, "I got to get out of this apartment, Father. *I got to get out of here!*"

There were two patrolmen on either side of the stoop. Captain Frick had chosen them from his ranks, had chosen four of his best shots, and then they had gone to Lieutenant Byrnes for their instructions. Their instructions were simple. Shoot to kill.

And so they waited on either side of the doorway now, four marksmen with their pistols drawn, waiting for something to happen.

From the first-floor windows of the tenement, Miranda's voice came.

"Lieutenant!"

"*Yes?*"

"This is Miranda! I've got the priest. I'm coming out."

"*What do you mean, Miranda? You're giving up?*"

"Giving up, my ass! The priest is coming out with me. If you've got any cops in the hallway, you'd better get them out now. You hear me?"

"It's gonna work," Parker whispered to Byrnes.

"*There are no policemen in the hallway, Miranda.*"

"There better not be. I want a clear path when I come out. This priest is staying with me all the way. Anybody so much as looks cockeyed at me, the priest gets it."

"*I thought you made a promise, Miranda.*"

"Don't make me laugh! I'm coming out."

Byrnes put down the megaphone and quickly drew his revolver. He turned slightly, so that his body hid the revolver which hung in his hand alongside his right thigh. Parker drew his gun, too, and then looked around for a good spot from which to fire. Behind the squad car? No, no. There! There was a place! The packing crate over there. He pushed his way through the crowd and climbed onto the crate. He checked the chambers of his .38, wiped his upper lip, and then faced the doorway. The street was very silent now. Upstairs, inside the building, they could hear a door slamming.

"Any cops in the hallway?" Miranda shouted. "Any cops here?"

There was no answer. Standing, watching the doorway, watching the patrolmen flanking the stoop, Byrnes thought, *All he has to do is turn his head. He'll see the patrolmen, and he'll put a bullet in Steve's back. That's all he has to do.* Patiently, Byrnes held his breath.

"I got the priest," Miranda shouted from the hallway. "Don't try nothing, you hear?"

The crowd had turned toward the doorway to the building. They could see nothing beyond the door. The hallway was dark, and the bright sunshine did not reach beyond the flat top step of the stoop.

"Clear a path!" Miranda shouted. "Clear a path, or I'll shoot into the crowd! I don't care who gets hurt!"

The crowd could see a pair of figures in the hallway now, dimly. The ~~priest~~ CARELLA was almost invisible because of ~~his~~ THE black cassock, but Miranda could be seen fairly clearly, a short thin man in a white undershirt. They hesitated in the vestibule, and Miranda peered past Carella's shoulder and into the street.

Zip pushed his way through the crowd with Cooch. The street was terribly silent, and he wanted to know why. What the hell was happening? He was angry because they'd been unable to locate China, angry because he wanted this Alfredo Gomez thing to end now, angry because things seemed to be going wrong, and he wanted them to go right. But, in spite of his anger, he was curious. The silence intrigued him. He pushed up to the barricade just as Carella and Miranda came onto the front stoop.

Miranda's eyes flicked the street. He was partially covered by the priest, so that a shot from across the street could not be risked. That left only . . .

And Miranda turned to look to the left of the stoop.

Carella was ready. He'd been waiting for the movement ever since they'd left the apartment. He'd been wondering where he would look if he were Miranda, and he'd realized that nobody could shoot from the other side of the street, and so any trap would have to be set on this side of the street, any shots would have to come from behind.

So Carella knew that Miranda knew, and he'd been waiting for the sideward movement of Miranda's head because he had further reasoned that Miranda would begin shooting the second he saw the cops on either side of the stoop.

Zip saw the cops the same moment Miranda did. It was too late to shout a warning.

Carella felt Miranda's head and eyes flickering to the left.

Go! he told himself.

He went.

No one said a word. Miranda turned toward Carella in the same instant that Carella threw himself headlong down the flight of steps.

And then the shooting started.

17

"Pepe!" Zip yelled. "Pepe!" But he was too late.

The crossfire was true crossfire. Miranda whirled to the left, and the bullets suddenly smashed into him from the right side of the stoop, spinning him around. He slammed into the railing and fired a shot at the patrolman who seemed closest to him, and then suddenly there were shots on his left, and he realized he was caught in a deadly crossfire, and he ran off the stoop toward where Carella lay sprawled at the foot of the steps. Byrnes began firing from the other side of the street, and Parker began firing from the crate, and then it seemed that every cop on that block had been waiting for just this moment because the street suddenly reverberated with ear-shattering sound as the bullets caromed into the gutter.

He seemed to be bleeding from a dozen places.

The white undershirt seemed to sprout blood like poppies in an instant. His own gun kept bucking in his hand, but there was blood dripping from his face and into his eyes, and he just fired blindly and sort of groped out toward the crowd as if he were reaching for salvation and didn't know whose face held it.

Parker came down off the crate, his service revolver trembling in his hand. The cops on the rooftops stopped firing all at once, and the men behind Miranda stopped firing as he stumbled blindly across the street, moving toward Parker who was similarly drawn toward him. It was almost as if someone had placed two magnetic figures on a long table. They moved toward each other inexorably, Miranda blinded by blood, and Parker drawn into that street by something he would never understand.

Miranda's gun clicked empty, and he looked at Parker in supplication, blood dripping into his eyes and bubbling out of his mouth, the mouth open, the hands limp now, the head twisted to one side like a Christ who had climbed down from the cross.

"Give me a break," Miranda whispered.

And Parker fired.

His shot took Miranda in the throat at close range, nearly ripping away the back of his neck. A fresh blossom of blood erupted, exposing Miranda's windpipe as he staggered forward again. His voice bubbled from his torn throat, a whispered voice that sounded as if it were coming from one of those trick underwater recording chambers, a voice directed only to Parker, a voice that sought out Parker on that spinning red street.

"Can't you ... can't you give me a break?" And again Parker fired. And this time, he kept his finger on the trigger, tightening the pressure each time a slug roared from the barrel of the gun, watching the slugs rip into Miranda, watching Miranda topple into the gutter lifelessly, and then standing over him and pumping bullets into his body until his gun was empty, and then grabbing a gun from the patrolman standing next to him and beginning to fire at the dead Miranda.

"That's enough," Carella shouted.

Zip pushed past the barricade and flung himself at Parker's back. Parker brushed him off like a pesky fly, swinging his huge shoulders, knocking Zip to the pavement.

"Leave him alone!" Zip shouted. "Leave him alone!"

But Parker was hearing nothing. He fired the patrolman's gun at Miranda's head, and then he fired again, and he was preparing to fire a third time when Carella grabbed his arms and pulled him away from the body.

"Somebody get up there to Frankie!" Lieutenant Byrnes shouted. "On the double!"

Two patrolmen rushed into the tenement. Byrnes walked over to Miranda and stared down at him.

"Is he dead?" a reporter called.

Byrnes nodded. There was no triumph in his voice. "He's dead."

"They killed him," Zip said to Cooch. "They killed him. The bastards killed him." He clutched Cooch frantically. "Where's Sixto? Where's Papá? We're gonna get him now, you hear me, Cooch? They killed Pepe, Cooch. You understand that? They killed him!" His eyes were wild. A thin layer of sweat covered his entire face.

"What about China?" Cooch asked. "You said we needed China to..."

"The hell with China! Alfie's gonna get his, you hear?"

A patrolman appeared on the fire escape. The street went quiet. He walked to where Frankie Hernandez lay still and silent, and he knelt down, and Byrnes waited. The patrolman stood up.

"Lieutenant?"

"Yes?"

"Frankie." The patrolman paused. "He's dead, sir."

Byrnes nodded. He nodded again. And then he realized the patrolman was waiting for instructions and, still nodding, he said, "Bring him down. Off there. Off the fire escape. Would you ... would you bring him down, please?"

The reporters had pushed past the barricade now, and they surrounded the body of the dead Miranda. Flash bulbs popped on the street, challenging the sunshine.

"Where's Sixto and Papá?" Zip asked. "Didn't I say to meet me here?"

"Look, Zip, calm down. Try to..."

"Don't tell me what to do!" Zip shouted, shaking Cooch's hand loose. "I know what I'm..." and he stopped talking.

Sixto and Papá had turned the corner, but it was not *their* appearance which had caused the sudden widening of Zip's eyes. He stared at the two boys and then he stared at their companion, and he balled his fists, because the person with them was Alfredo Gomez.

"Wha—?" he started, and in that instant two patrolmen came from the doorway of the tenement, carrying the body of Frankie Hernandez on a stretcher. The people in the crowd began murmuring his name as the body went past. Handkerchiefs appeared, and women sniffled into them. The men in the crowd were taking off their hats and holding them to their chests.

"It's Frankie," Luís said. "Close the doors! For respect! For respect!" He reached up for the overhead door of the luncheonette and pulled it down. On the avenue side of the shop another man pulled down the door there, so that the shop faced the street blindly – *We will not conduct business while you pass by, my friend* – as the patrolmen carried the body of Hernandez toward the ambulance.

"Can we get a few more pictures of Miranda, Lieutenant?" one of the reporters asked.

"Take all the pictures you want," Byrnes said. "He's in no hurry. Not any more."

Luís rolled back the doors. The shop was open again.

"What happens now, Lieutenant?" the reporter asked.

Byrnes sighed heavily. "We pile him in the meat wagon, and we cart him off. I get my men off the streets. Try to unsnarl the traffic. And then take up a collection for a good cop. I don't know. What happens next?" He turned to Carella. "Steve?"

"Yeah?"

"Who's gonna tell Frankie's father? Who's gonna go into that candy store around the corner, where he's got Frankie's picture pasted to the mirror, who's gonna go in there and tell him Frankie is dead?"

"I'll do it if you like, Pete."

"No," Byrnes said, sighing and shaking his head. "It's my job."

"We really nailed him, didn't we?" Parker said, striding over. "We really nailed the son of a—"

"Shut up, Parker!" Byrnes snapped.

"Wh—?"

"Shut your goddamn mouth!"

"Wh–what the hell is wrong *now*?" Parker asked, his face taking on a hurt and astonished look.

Sixto, Papá, and Alfredo stood near the luncheonette. Zip walked to them quickly.

"What is this, Sixto?" he asked.

"What do you think it is, Zip?"

"I don't like guessing games. What are you up to?"

"I tell you, Zip," Sixto said simply. "If you wann to kill Alfredo, you got to kill us all."

"What the hell are you talking about, you meatball?"

"I say it pretty plain, Zip."

"You know me an' Cooch are heeled? You know we can blast you all over the sidewalk?"

"*Sí*, we know," Sixto said. "Go ahead. Blast us all ov' the sidewalk."

"What do you . . .?" Zip stopped and looked into Sixto's eyes. Slightly unnerved, he said, "What do you – mean?"

"Be careful, Zip," Cooch said quickly. "They got something up their sleeves. I can see it. They're too . . . they're too sure of themselves."

"Sixto's got them buffaloed," Zip said quickly. He turned his attention to Papá. "You're on the wrong side, Papá. You stick with Sixto, and it's like siding with the ones who killed Pepe. You'd be..."

"Pepe brings disgrace to the *barrio*," Papá said.

"All right, that's enough pictures," Byrnes shouted. "Let's get him out of here, huh?"

Two patrolmen reached down and rolled Miranda onto a stretcher. Another patrolman threw a blanket over him. Gingerly, they stepped around the pool of blood in the gutter and began moving toward the luncheonette.

"The doors!" Zip shouted. "Close the doors for him!"

But no one moved toward the doors. Instead, the people in the street watched the body as it passed by, and slowly, one by one, they turned their backs to it, so that the body, as the cops carried it toward the luncheonette, was presented with a solid wall of denial.

"The doors!" Zip shouted again. "We should close the doors!"

But no one moved. One by one, they denied the body of Miranda, and then – silently, so silently – they began moving off the street. What had been a milling, shouting mob not ten minutes ago was suddenly a dispersing group of whispering people, and then not even a group any more, simply a few stragglers, people in twos and threes; and then the street barricades were carted away, and the squad cars revved their engines, and the street seemed to settle down into its Sunday niche again, quiet, peaceful. It almost seemed as if nothing had happened on that street that day.

Zip stood before the opened doors and watched the body of Miranda shoved into the ambulance, and then he whirled toward Sixto and shouted, "You think you're gonna get away with this?"

"Move aside, Zip," Sixto said calmly. "We wann to get through now."

"You won't be able to walk the street no more!" Zip shouted. "You think you..."

"We'll see," Sixto said, and the three boys stepped away from the luncheonette, and walked past Zip and Cooch who did not move to stop them.

"You're making a mistake!" Zip yelled after them. "You're making a *big mistake!*" But he did not run after them, and he did not try to stop them. "Why didn't you help me, Cooch?" he said suddenly, angrily. "For Christ's sake, we just let them walk *away*, for Christ's sake!"

"They're ... they're too strong, Zip," Cooch said in a whisper.

"We're the ones with the guns!" Zip protested.

"Yeah, but ... they ... they were strong," Cooch said, and his voice fell.

"Aw—" Zip made a meaningless little gesture with his right hand. "Aw—" He stared off down the street. The squad cars had pulled away now. Patrolmen were still lingering on the block, but most of the police were gone. The street stretched ahead in sticky blackness washed with hot sunshine. On the avenue, the traffic had started up again. "Jesus, what a ... what a miserable day this turned out to be," Zip said, and he looked at Cooch with troubled eyes.

"Yeah," Cooch said softly.

Zip looked back at the street, and then he sighed heavily. "Well ... what do you want to do the ... the rest of the afternoon, Cooch?"

"I don't know," Cooch said.

"Ain't you ... ain't you got no ideas?"

"We could go to the flicks, I guess."

"Yeah," Zip said emptily.

"Or play some stickball, maybe."

"Yeah."

"Maybe go for a swim at the pool."

"Yeah. Yeah, maybe we could do that." He turned his head

suddenly and jerkily because he did not want Cooch to see the tears that had sprung into his eyes. Nor did he know why he was crying. It was just that, all at once, in the heart of one of the biggest cities in the world, Zip had felt all alone, utterly alone, and the enormity of the city and the inconsequence of himself had – had suddenly frightened him.

"I guess – I guess we'll find something," he said, and he thrust his hands into his pockets, and the two boys walked up the sun-drenched street, their heads bent.

Andy Parker passed them on his way to the luncheonette. He glanced at them, shrugged, and went in to say hello to his friend Luís.

"You still sore at me, Luís?" he asked, as if this had been troubling him all along, as if it were important for him to know that Luís was not angry.

"No, Andy," Luís said.

"Everybody's sore at me," Parker said blankly. He paused. "Why's everybody sore at me?" He paused again. "I do my job." He looked up at Luís. "I'm sorry I yelled at you, Luís."

"It doesn't matter."

"Well, I'm sorry."

He stared at Luís. And because Luís was a human being, and because apologies are never sincere unless they are tested, unless someone hurls into the face of "I'm sorry," the unforgiving reply, "who cares whether you're sorry or not? Go drop dead in a corner!" and gets one or two further responses. Gets, "In any case, I really am sorry," or gets, "Well if that's the way you feel, go to hell!" and knows by these further responses whether the apology was real to begin with, being human, Luís tested the apology.

"You should have thought of that before you spoke," he said, and his eyes narrowed, and he waited for Parker's answer.

Parker nodded. "I should have," Parker agreed. "I'm sorry."

The men stared at each other. There was nothing further to

say for now. Perhaps there was nothing further to say *ever*.

"Well, I ... I better get back to the squad," Parker said.

"*Sí*."

Parker waved, seemed to become embarrassed in the middle of the gesture, and let his hand drop. Slowly, he shuffled off up the street.

A reporter walked into the luncheonette and took a stool. "Well, everything quiet again, huh?" he said. "Let me have a cup of coffee, huh?"

"*Sí*, everything quiet," Luís answered.

"Just like the island, huh?" the reporter said.

Instantly, Luís answered, "No, not just like the island," and then he paused, and then he looked at the reporter, and then he said, "But maybe not so bad anyway, eh? Maybe not so bad."

Down the street, the church bells began tolling.

Other titles by Ed McBain and available from Hodder and Stoughton

All these books are available at your local bookshop or newsagent, or can be ordered direct from the publisher. Just tick the titles you want and fill in the form below.

Prices and availability subject to change without notice.

HODDER AND STOUGHTON PAPERBACKS, P.O. Box 11, Falmouth, Cornwall.

Please send cheque or postal order for the value of the book, and add the following for postage and packing.

UK including BFPO – £1.00 for one book, plus 50p for the second book, and 30p for each additional book ordered up to a £3.00 maximum.

OVERSEAS INCLUDING EIRE – £2.00 for the first book, plus £1.00 for the second book, and 50p for each additional book ordered.

OR Please debit this amount from my Access/Visa Card (delete as appropriate).

Card Number ☐☐☐☐☐☐☐☐☐☐☐☐☐☐☐☐☐☐

AMOUNT £ ....

EXPIRY DATE ....

SIGNED ....

NAME ....

ADDRESS ....

....

WE CAN BE HEROES,
JUST FOR ONE DAY . . .

The Dreams . . .

Brian Doyle, the Yankees' journeyman second base-man with a .161 career batting average, who subbed for an injured starter in the 1978 World Series . . . and siz-zled at the plate, going an astonishing 7 for 16!

Mini Roberts, the four-feet, eleven-inch, 66-year-old who took a long shot at the Michigan state women's weightlifting title . . . and won!

The Disasters . . .

Roy Riegels, who recovered a fumble in the 1929 Rose Bowl game and ran it 60 yards downfield . . . into the wrong end zone!

Eddie "The Eagle" Edwards, the plucky English plasterer who made it all the way to the 1988 Olympic ski jump competition, winning the hearts of millions . . . and finishing dead last!

And The Truly Bizarre . . .

Jeffrey Maier, the 12-year-old Yankee fan sitting be-hind the right field wall at game one of the American League Championship, who reached into the field of play to snag a Derek Jeter fly ball, robbing the Orioles outfielder standing below of a fair catch!

Eddie Gaedel, who came up to bat only once for the St. Louis Browns and walked . . . due to the fact that he was only three-and-a-half feet tall!

ATTENTION: ORGANIZATIONS AND CORPORATIONS
Most HarperTorch paperbacks are available at special quantity discounts for bulk purchases for sales promotions, premiums, or fund-raising. For information, please call or write:

Special Markets Department, HarperCollins Publishers, Inc., 10 East 53rd Street, New York, N.Y. 10022–5299.
Telephone: (212) 207–7528. Fax: (212) 207–7222.